Cathy looked across at Pearce and her heart twisted

She had fallen for him but how it had happened she didn't know. All she knew was that she loved him with every fiber of her soul. She needed to tell him the truth about herself. Her article for the paper was unimportant, compared with the depth of feeling inside her.

If she told him now, what would his reaction be? she wondered. Obviously he would be livid to begin with, but whether he would forgive her or not was down to how much he felt for her.

He was watching her silently and she knew that her confusion—her indecision—was there for him to see.

Dear Reader,

A perfect nanny can be tough to find, but once you've found her you'll love and treasure her forever. She's someone who'll not only look after the kids but could also be that loving mom they never knew. Or sometimes she's a he and is the daddy they are wishing for.

Here at Harlequin Presents we've put together a compelling new series, NANNY WANTED!, in which some of our most popular authors create nannies whose talents extend way beyond taking care of the children! Each story will excite and delight you and make you wonder how any family could be complete without a nineties nanny.

Remember—Nanny knows best when it comes to falling in love!

The Editors

Look out next month for:
A NANNY NAMED NICK by Miranda Lee
(#1943)

KATHRYN ROSS

The Love-Child

Harlequin Books

TORONTO • NEW YORK • LONDON
AMSTERDAM • PARIS • SYDNEY • HAMBURG
STOCKHOLM • ATHENS • TOKYO • MILAN
MADRID • WARSAW • BUDAPEST • AUCKLAND

ISBN 0-373-11938-0

THE LOVE-CHILD

First North American Publication 1998.

Printed in U.S.A.

CHAPTER ONE

THE French Riviera shimmered in blistering heat. Cathy lay on a sun-lounger next to the pool at her hotel and tried to gather up the energy to move into the shade.

This was really quite blissful, she told herself dreamily. Coming away on holiday on her own wasn't as awful as she had feared; it was a chance to recharge her batteries. London and her job at the newspaper had been getting very hectic, very stressful.

No sooner had the thought crossed her mind than she was interrupted by a waiter, telling her there that there was a phone call for her.

'For me? Are you sure?' She frowned and swung long shapely legs over the side of the lounger, drawing admiring glances from two men who were sitting at the pool bar.

'Definitely for you, Mademoiselle Fielding,' the waiter said patiently.

'OK, *merci*.' Brushing her long blonde hair back from her face with impatient fingers, she took the cordless phone from him.

'Cathy, it's Mike. Have I got news for you,' a cheerful voice boomed down the line, sending ominous shivers down her back.

It was her editor, Mike Johnson. Forty-five, crusty and as hard as nails. He sounded far too cheerful for her liking. 'Only if the premises have burnt down or the Prime Minister has run off with a nun can this phone call be justified, Mike,' she told him straight. She didn't want to be reminded of work...it wasn't fair. Everyone was entitled to a vacation.

'Come on, Cathy, I'll lay money on the fact that you are bored to tears and just dying to get back to work,' her editor shot back quickly. 'I know you. You're a damn good journalist and you are never happier than when I give you a good assignment. You'd rather be in the pouring rain with a good story than sunning yourself in the South of France.'

'Dream on,' Cathy murmured abrasively.

Mike continued as if she hadn't spoken. 'I've got a real scoop and it's right on your doorstep.'

There was a brief pause while Cathy fought with herself not to ask. She bit down on her lip but the words refused to be held back. 'So, what is it?'

'Pearce Tyrone is staying at his villa...just down the road from your hotel.'

'So?' Cathy frowned. 'What's the big deal? He's a successful writer; I'm sure he stays at his French home a lot.'

'Jody Sterling's child has been sent to him. It's all strictly hush-hush and as yet none of the other papers are on to it—'

'How reliable is your information?' she interrupted swiftly.

'Very.' He emphasised the word heavily. 'I have it on good authority that little Poppy arrived at the Tyrone house early this morning.'

Cathy felt a flicker of interest. Jody Sterling had been all over the newspapers recently, having had a near-fatal car accident. She was a phenomenally talented actress. Blonde and beautiful, she was frequently the centre of a lot of media attention, but never more so than when she had given birth to an illegitimate child nine months previously and had refused to name the father.

Speculation had been rife. *Cê Va* magazine had featured the actress on the arm of prominent, married politician Jonathan Briars and the scandal had deepened to almost ruin the man's career. The other name to be linked with the actress was Pearce Tyrone.

Pearce was an enigma. No one knew much about the thirty-seven-year-old except that he was an exceptionally successful author, persistently in the bestseller list. Cathy had seen his photograph on only a few occasions when someone had surreptitiously managed to snap him leaving a restaurant or hotel.

The man shunned interviews and refused to let a journalist within striking distance. He held his privacy like a dark protective cloak around him. There was no information about his life on the covers of his books, and no photograph—even though he had the fabulous dark looks of an Adonis. The more he refused to be drawn into giving an interview the more interested the public became in him.

Was he the father of Jody Sterling's baby? The question hovered tantalisingly in Cathy's mind.

'Well are you interested?' Mike's gruff voice interrupted her thoughts.

'It's certainly juicy,' Cathy murmured. 'But it's hardly my line, Mike. You know I like harder news…scandal and tittle-tattle are more up Linda Hardman's street.'

'Linda's in New York. You are on the spot.' Mike's voice rasped harshly, all hint of amusement gone. 'And, anyway, the French air-traffic controllers went out on strike last night; I can't get anyone there quick enough. You'll have to step in. Get down there and interview him before the other papers get wind of it.'

'Hey, give me a break!' she howled. 'This is a guy who thinks that even a book-signing session is an invasion of privacy. How will I get an interview?'

'Use your initiative; you're good at that.' Her boss's voice brooked no argument. 'Oh, and don't forget to take pictures…. I'm relying on you.' Then, in a deeper, more sinister tone, he added, 'Your job's relying on it.'

The line went dead at that.

Oh, wonderful, Cathy thought as she put down the receiver. There was nothing like finishing with an ultimatum. Totally unnecessary, she decided with a shake of her head, but, then, that was Mike all over—he liked the forceful approach. He would be laughing with glee now at the thought of her sitting outside Pearce Tyrone's gates, desperate to get in.

Just under an hour later Cathy drove her hire car along the Corniche in search of Pearce Tyrone's villa.

She had asked at the hotel and one of the receptionists had told her that it was along here somewhere, hidden behind huge gates with stone lions on pillars at either side. She slowed down, scanning the abundant greenery that covered the mountainous slopes. No houses were visible from the road; they were all well hidden behind a profusion of trees and shrubs.

She rounded a very sharp bend and then suddenly saw the gates up ahead. There was no mistaking them, tall and imposing with lions at either side, looking proudly out across the blue of the Mediterranean Sea.

She pulled the car in to the side of the road and sat looking at the gates, her heart thudding nervously. Now she had to fathom out how to gain access.

One good thing was the fact that there was nobody else around. Either the other members of the press hadn't got wind of the developments here or Mike's information was wrong. She studied the gates with anxious eyes. They were obviously electronically operated and there were cameras pointing down from either side of the pillars. That didn't bode well for an easy entry.

Cathy bit down on the softness of her lips. She could drive up there and try the direct approach—'I'm here to interview Mr Tyrone'—then get sent away with a curt 'get lost' ringing in her ears. Or she could try the more devious tactic of a woman in distress. Not a very virtuous ploy but it might get her through the gates. She turned the rear-view mirror and checked her appearance.

Cool emerald-green eyes, fringed with long dark lashes, stared back at her from a heart-shaped face. She put a hand to her honey-blonde hair, wondering if she should take it out of the rather severe plait that held it back from her face. Her hair was her crowning glory, long, thick and naturally blonde; it always got her noticed. At the office they had nicknamed her 'Barbie' because of her hair and shapely figure. It was a nickname that irritated Cathy intensely; sometimes she felt that because she was blonde with long legs her work was not taken seriously enough.

However, there were times when looking glamorous had its advantages and this could be one of them. She could effect a pouty and breathy helplessness at the gates and say that there was something wrong with her car, then ask to use their phone. Her hand paused on the velvet tie that held her hair neatly in place, and suddenly she thought better of the idea. No, she wouldn't stoop so low...she would get this interview fair and square.

With determination, she put the car into gear and moved slowly forward towards the gates. As she'd suspected, the cameras were immediately trained on her as she stopped and wound down her car window.

'Please state your business,' a male voice ordered in broken English over a crackling intercom.

For a fraction of a second she hesitated and then stated with perfect confidence, 'I'm here to see Mr. Tyrone.'

There was a moment's silence and then, to her absolute amazement, the voice issued the command for her to enter and the large gates ground slowly open in front of her.

There you are, she told herself crisply as she drove through; honesty is always the best policy. Even as she spoke the words she had the feeling that something wasn't right here. This was just too easy.

Cautiously she proceeded up the long winding driveway and when the pretty pink villa came into view, with its dark green shutters still tightly closed against the heat of the sun, she drew in her breath with delight. There was nothing ostentatious about the place, yet it was simply perfect—an oasis of peaceful beauty, surrounded by trees and beautiful flowers. Terracotta pots filled with bright red geraniums lined the steps up to a front door which had been left invitingly open.

What more could I ask? Cathy thought with glee as she parked the car and stepped out into the warm air, fragrant with geraniums and lavender. She ran a smoothing hand over her white linen sun-dress as she slowly walked towards the door. Now all she had to decide was what track her interview should follow. Should she start by asking Tyrone outright if he was the father of Jody Sterling's child? Or should she word the question differently—just ask if the actress had officially named him as the child's next of kin? Her thoughts were interrupted by the appearance of Pearce Tyrone himself on the front steps.

Hell! He's gorgeous! Cathy's business-like thoughts disintegrated as her gaze met with flint-like sapphire-blue eyes. It was totally out of character but her mind went completely blank and her senses were sent into chaos as she noted the powerful breadth of his shoulders, the elegant cut of his summer suit.

He was nine years her senior at thirty-seven, and six feet two with ruggedly handsome good looks and jet black hair. The few photographs she had seen of him had prepared her for the fact that he was attractive, but what she hadn't expected was the magnetising power of his looks. But there was something else as well. It was really very strange, but she almost felt as if she knew him—as if they had met before somewhere. Yet she knew for certain that they hadn't.

'Where the hell have you been?' he rasped angrily. 'I've been expecting you for hours.'

Cathy could do nothing but stare at him, totally taken aback by his sudden outburst.

His eyes raked her face impatiently. Then suddenly he frowned. 'You are from the agency?' His voice deepened ominously and his eyes moved, taking in every detail of her shapely figure in the white dress.

The tone of his voice left Cathy in no doubt that if she didn't just say yes he would throw her bodily back out onto the road.

She gave a slight nod, although what she was agreeing to she had no idea. All she could think of was that she didn't want to spoil her chances of getting through his front door.

'Thank heaven for that.' He waved a hand rather imperiously for her to proceed with him into the house. 'The child hasn't stopped crying for hours.' His voice grated with a mixture of anxiety and annoyance.

Cathy searched for something intelligent and noncommittal to say...nothing came to mind. All she could think of was that he had verified that there was a child here. Silently she walked ahead of him and then stood aside as he closed the front door behind them and pulled a heavy bolt across it.

Too late, Cathy found herself thinking sardonically as she glanced around the gracious hallway. The stranger from the press had already entered the lion's den. She shivered as she glanced back and met those deep blue eyes head on again. She just hoped that the lion wouldn't eat her alive when he discovered the truth.

'Did the agency fill you in with the details?' He glared at her.

Nerves twisted and spiralled as she wondered what on earth he was talking about. She gave a brief nod.

'Good. I'll take you straight up to Poppy,' he said grimly. 'We can get down to business later.'

Better and better, Cathy thought as she followed him up a curving staircase with wrought-iron banisters. Or perhaps she should say curiouser and curiouser. Mike Johnson wasn't going to believe her luck. And obviously her editor's information had been quite correct. Jody Sterling's child was here.

Pearce led her swiftly down a long corridor and it was then that she first heard the muffled cry of a child. As they approached the room at the end the crying grew louder until—when he opened the door—the full wail of the infant's lungs ripped the air apart.

The room was primrose-yellow, the sprigged white muslin curtains moved gently in the soft breeze from the open window and in the centre of the room a middle-aged man was bending over a cot, trying to soothe a distressed child. When they entered he turned towards them a relieved look on his lined face.

'*Au secours, ça suffit!*' He spoke in deep rapid French, his eyes darting from Pearce to Cathy, his manner clearly agitated.

'Don't worry, Henri. You did what you could and I am most grateful. But the nanny is here now, and she will take care of things.'

Pearce's voice was rich, dark and hypnotically authoritative. Cathy looked behind her to see where the nanny was. Anyone who could quieten this child had her full admiration. Suddenly her spirits sank as reality dawned. He was talking about her! Somehow he had mistakenly taken her for the child's nanny!

'Well don't just stand there.' Pearce Tyrone's voice lifted derisively as the child seemed to bellow even more furiously, her breath catching painfully.

It crossed Cathy's mind to just come clean with the truth—tell him that she didn't know anything about babies and that she was from the press.

She looked into Pearce Tyrone's eyes. They seemed to have darkened to deepest midnight, his lips set in a grim, uncompromising line. Maybe the truth could wait, she countered hastily. Once told, her feet wouldn't touch the ground, and before leaving she should at least try to find out something about this situation. Get some angle for a good story.

As the older man left the room, still noisily bemoaning his failure with his charge, Cathy moved over to the side of the cot and looked down at the child—trying to guess what was causing her so much distress. Perhaps she was hungry or needed to be changed?

Cathy racked her brains. She had done an article on modern-day child care not so long ago; she had done a lot of research for it, but unfortunately it had been more theoretical than practical.

'She has cried almost continually since she arrived today,' Pearce informed her, an edge of strain clear in his voice. 'I've been worried sick.'

Cathy glanced at him, an expression of genuine sympathy in her eyes. She remembered her sister telling her how distressed she had felt when her young daughter had suffered from colic and had cried almost continuously.

The infant let out a particularly loud wail and Pearce Tyrone crossed to stand next to her at the cot. 'I've tried holding her over my shoulder, feeding her, changing her, and still she cries.' He raked a hand through the thickness of his dark hair. 'I've never felt so damn helpless.'

Cathy's eyebrows lifted a little. It was amazing that one small baby could reduce such a powerful, dominant male into making such a statement. She was willing to

bet her last franc on the fact that nothing had ever made
Pearce Tyrone feel helpless before.

Tentatively Cathy put out a hand and gently stroked
the infant's brow. Magically the sobbing lessened as
though the child had recognised the touch of her hand.
Quick to press her advantage, Cathy leaned down and
crooned close to her ear. 'What's the matter, then, sweetheart?'

The little face turned briefly to look at her. It was red
from crying and Cathy felt a rush of tenderness that almost choked her. Almost at once the child started to cry
again with renewed vigour, pushing the back of her
small dimpled hands into her eyes.

Poor little thing, Cathy thought sadly. She had expected to see her mother and instead she had found another stranger.

'Would you like to come out of that nasty cot and
have a little cuddle, then?' Cathy coaxed gently and
reached in to gather up the wriggling flurry of cherubic
arms and legs. Carefully she supported the child's back
and head until she had her safely in her arms. The crying
stopped almost immediately and a pair of speedwell-blue
eyes, fringed with dark curly lashes, looked up into
Cathy's face in astonishment. The relief of silence was
heady.

'What was all that noise about, then?' Cathy asked
softly, placing a playful finger under the baby's chin.
She was only about nine months old and very beautiful.
Immediately the child's small fingers encircled Cathy's
and held on for dear life, as though frightened she was
going to be left alone once more.

For a moment the importance of getting a story from
Pearce Tyrone paled under the awful fact that this child
might lose her mother. Jody Sterling was in a coma in
hospital in Paris and might never recover. Perhaps this
was a contributing factor to Tyrone's obvious distress.

She had obviously caught the man in a rare unguarded moment of stress, otherwise she would never have got past the front gate. With a bit of luck she could admit to him now that she wasn't really a nanny and he would be so grateful to her that he would grant her a full interview.

'Poppy seems to have taken a liking to you, Miss...?'

Cathy hesitated just a fraction of a second before giving him her real name. 'Fielding...Cathy Fielding.'

He frowned and the handsome face took on a very stern expression, the sort of look that—in Cathy's experience—preceded being forcefully ejected from a situation.

'That's not the name the agency sent... I was expecting someone called Mabel...something or other.'

There was the briefest pause before Cathy found herself lying blatantly. 'Mabel is my real name, but I never use it.' She opened her eyes in a wide, coquettish way. 'I don't think it's very attractive, do you?'

He looked at her as if she had suddenly grown two heads. 'Frankly, I haven't the inclination to ponder on things of such magnitude,' he told her derisively.

His tone, his expression, was like a cool slap across the face. Feeling totally put down, Cathy felt a flare of anger rise. This man took himself far too seriously.

'All I care about is whether you are as highly qualified as the agency has led me to believe,' he continued briskly.

Qualified to write a story that would open the public's eyes to the real Pearce Tyrone, she told herself firmly. Given just a little time inside this house, she might gather enough information to warm Mike's heart. A gleam of devilment lit the wide beauty of her eyes. 'Oh, I'm very highly qualified,' she assured him.

The baby wriggled slightly in her arms and then

reached up one little hand and grabbed at a loose tendril of Cathy's hair with a grip that was surprisingly strong.

'Ow!' It took a moment to gently extricate herself and then Poppy reached her arms towards Pearce, a sweet smile on her little face.

Looking over at Pearce, Cathy noticed that the remote countenance with which he had regarded her had softened to tenderness as he studied the child.

'So, why didn't you behave for me and Henri?' he asked Poppy playfully. 'How come you only respond to a woman?'

The child chuckled and looked as if she understood every word that he spoke.

Cathy smiled and then risked commenting, 'Perhaps I remind her of her mother? We've got the same colour hair, haven't we?'

Cathy knew at that moment how Pearce had got his name. Those eyes seemed to slice through her. He made no effort to reply and the silence and the way he was looking at her was very unnerving.

Was this the moment when he threw her bodily from the premises? she wondered. Well, she wouldn't go without giving this her best shot. 'I...I know I'm not as glamorous as Jody Sterling; she's very beautiful. Poppy looks a little like her, though, don't you think?' She rocked the child gently and then cut straight to the bottom line. 'Or perhaps you think she looks more like you?'

Cathy tried very hard to glean something from his expression, but it was hard to tell what was going on behind that cool mask of indifference. His lips curved and she imagined there was a faint, barely discernible hint of contempt. Then he merely shrugged and answered laconically, 'If you say so, Ms. Fielding...if you say so.'

She frowned. 'But what do you think?'

One dark eyebrow lifted. 'I think that I haven't got time to stand discussing such nonsense with a member of staff.'

Now she knew that she hadn't imagined that look of contempt. The tone...the manner were all very definitely condescending. Obviously Pearce Tyrone didn't just keep the media at bay; he kept himself loftily apart from most people...depending on their social standing, of course. He was a snob, an arrogant snob who erected social barriers...who would never be found fraternising with staff! Fury blazed through her at such pomposity.

'Your bedroom is through there.' Pearce waved a hand airily towards a connecting door. 'Shall I get Henri to bring in your luggage from your car?'

This succeeded in bringing her senses sharply back to the situation in hand. It seemed that the nanny was to live in and if Tyrone discovered she had no luggage his suspicions would be aroused. 'Uh...no.... I can manage perfectly, thank you.' Her heart thudded uncomfortably as she wondered how long she could possibly get away with this and where the real nanny was.

'OK.' He glanced at his watch. 'Attend to Poppy and then come down and see me in my study...say, ten minutes.' It wasn't a question, more a command. 'It's at the bottom of the stairs, first on the right.'

As he strode towards the door Cathy sank down on the chair beside her. Her legs felt decidedly shaky. She didn't like this one bit...she should never have let it go so far.

She was not a devious, underhanded type of person and this whole situation was way out of her usual league. She had never before pretended to be someone else in order to get a story. But it had just seemed so deliciously irresistible to follow this game wherever it might lead... Curiosity burnt inside her.

Cathy looked down at the baby, who was staring up at her with mesmerising blue eyes.

The child gurgled happily.

'Well might you laugh.' Cathy shook her head. She should have owned up; told the man who she was... Deceiving a man like Tyrone was asking for trouble. But she was inside his home...inside Pearce Tyrone's sacred domain where no reporter had walked before. The dramatic words rattled around her mind, making her smile.

She placed Poppy down on a changing mat on the floor and then reached into her handbag. A few quick photos were in order. It seemed very likely that the real nanny would turn up at any moment so she had better get what she could—and quickly.

CHAPTER TWO

THE room was very well equipped. Everything a baby could possibly need was there. With the imminent threat of discovery weighing heavily over her head, Cathy worked quickly. Several shots of the child, looking up at her in an adoring fashion. A few of the toys and the new clothes that filled the cupboards. They were all from the same, very chic, expensive shop in Nice, Cathy noted.

A noise in the corridor made her fling her camera back into her bag. She was only just in time. A few seconds later Henri came into the room.

'Having difficulty, *mademoiselle*?' he asked as he saw her standing beside the open cupboards.

'Just familiarising myself with everything,' she answered breezily.

He didn't look impressed. 'Mr Tyrone wants to see you in his study. I will watch Poppy.'

He sat on the chair just inside the door and crossed his arms. Watching her from beneath hooded eyelids.

Cathy found him a little disconcerting, but the scent of a promising story made her linger.

'Mr. Tyrone has been very busy,' she remarked nonchalantly, nodding towards all the cupboards. 'Did he go out and buy all these things when he heard about Ms Sterling's accident? Or did he have them here from the moment the child was born?'

Silence met the question and she turned enquiring eyes on the man. He just shrugged. 'I couldn't say, *mademoiselle*.'

Couldn't say, or wouldn't say? Irritated, Cathy moved further around the room and opened the connecting door.

Her eyes widened at the sight of a luxuriously beautiful bedroom. White carpets and turquoise silk covers on the four-poster bed gave it a very opulent air. Large picture windows gave panoramic views out over the sparkling blue of the Mediterranean.

She could see an *en suite* bathroom through another door beside the built-in wardrobes.

'Mr Tyrone believes in keeping his staff in luxury,' she murmured in total surprise.

'It is a guest room,' Henri murmured.

'I see.' Cathy turned and with a carefully polite smile she asked, 'Is this where Jody Sterling sleeps when she visits?'

The man looked at her sharply. 'This is a large house, *mademoiselle*; I do not know.' Then he glanced pointedly at his watch. 'You should not keep Monsieur Tyrone waiting.'

With a sigh, she turned from him. It was obvious that Henri wasn't going to be forthcoming. 'If you don't mind, I'll just freshen up,' she told him and headed into the bedroom, closing the door behind her.

Taking out her camera, she weighed up the possible photos she could take of the room. Then, before taking them, she walked across to the bathroom and turned on the taps in the wash basin, just to cover the sound of the camera's shutter.

At least she would have something to give Mike, she thought with some satisfaction a few moments later as she pushed the camera back in her bag and then went to turn the water off. Now all she had to do was try and get some unguarded comments from Tyrone himself.

She glanced at herself in the mirror and noticed that strands of her hair were in untidy straggles around her face where Poppy had managed to pull it free of its ties.

She grimaced. It might help matters if she looked reasonably tidy before facing the tyrant in his den.

Quickly she pulled her blonde hair free from its plait and drew a brush through its silken length.

Better, she smiled at her reflection. Pearce Tyrone would be easy, she told herself confidently.

She heard Tyrone's voice before she could see him. She followed the deep booming sound of his displeasure down the stairs. He sounded formidable, and with every step towards his office door she could feel her confidence faltering.

'Well, your agency assured me of a prompt service,' he was saying in an irate tone.

Somebody had well and truly rattled the man's cage, Cathy thought as she stopped in the doorway to his study. Her eyes scanned the room with professional interest, trying to store every detail while he was otherwise occupied.

He was sitting behind an enormous desk in a very beautiful room. The walls were covered in bookshelves and French doors looked out over a picturesque garden, lit by the rosy hue of evening. Beside him there was another desk with a computer and fax machine on it, and angled to one side was a coffee machine.

Pearce didn't see her immediately. His head was bent and he was raking one hand through his dark hair in an angry way as he listened to whoever was at the other end of the line. Cathy didn't envy whoever it was. She wouldn't want to be on the receiving end of Peace Tyrone's temper—he sounded most indomitable. She only hoped that she could get her story and be out of here before he discovered her deception.

'It's just not good enough. I pay good money and expect—' Pearce broke off as he looked up and caught sight of Cathy in the doorway.

His eyes moved over her from her shoes right the way over her body, studying her intently with a blatantly male interest. The in-depth scrutiny made her feel extremely self-conscious and there was the strangest feeling in the pit of her stomach, as if she had just stepped off a high diving board.

'Never mind.' Pearce continued abruptly now. 'Leave it. I'll phone you back.' Then he slammed down the phone.

'Problem?' Cathy asked with an innocent lift of one eyebrow.

'Nothing I can't handle.' Pearce's voice was crisp and businesslike, his expression remote and distinctly unfriendly, making Cathy wonder if she had imagined his earlier look of approval. 'You look different,' he said.

'Different?'

'Your hair,' he said curtly. 'You've left it loose.'

The way he spoke was almost like an accusation. 'Oh.' She put a hand awkwardly to the long honey gold length and tucked it behind her ears. 'Poppy had pulled it and I just thought I'd tidy up before coming down here.'

'Come in and sit down.' He cut across her rambling explanations and waved a hand imperiously towards the chair opposite him.

Feeling a bit like a child who had transgressed and had been summoned to the headmaster's office, Cathy obediently took her place opposite him. For a moment he didn't say anything—just looked at her. It took all of her self-control not to squirm uncomfortably under that probing stare.

He was examining her as a scientist would study something under a microscope, she thought angrily, as his eyes swept over her lightly tanned complexion, the heavy thickness of her hair and the scoop neckline of her white dress with deep contemplation.

'So,' he spoke sharply, 'you are Ms Cathy Fielding, nanny extraordinaire?'

'Well…I…I try my best.' She held his gaze with difficulty, trying not to feel intimidated by him. No one had ever made her feel so on edge before but, then, she had never pretended to be anything other than what she was before.

'Can you type?' he asked bluntly.

'Yes.' She inclined her head.

'Excellent.' He smiled at her, a warm smile that did very weird things to her pulse rate. His swings of mood were dizzying, she thought hazily. 'As you just overheard, my secretary has let me down. I've got a deadline to make with a book and I need someone to type up my notes.'

'That's no problem,' she assured him. In fact, it was probably the only thing that he needed that she was qualified to do.

'Right, let's take a look at your references.'

Her heart gave a double beat and she was just opening her mouth to make a feeble excuse for not having them with her when he leaned across to the filing cabinet next to him. 'They faxed them to me yesterday but, to be honest, I haven't had a chance to study them in depth.'

She watched, wide-eyed, as he pulled out a paper folder. 'The agency did speak very highly of you,' he told her.

'Did they?' She sounded as breathless as she felt. She waited helplessly as he pulled out the pages inside, knowing full well that as soon as he looked at them he would know that she was an impostor. For one thing, the wrong surname would be at the top of the page.

She coughed and then caught her breath. 'Do you think I could have a drink?' she asked in a desperate attempt to forestall him.

'Certainly.' He swivelled his leather chair towards the coffee machine behind him. 'Black all right?'

She didn't get a chance to answer because at that juncture the shrill ring of a bell split the silence of the house.

'Damn, someone is at the gate.' Pearce hesitated and then stood up. 'Excuse me a moment. I'd better see to it as Henri is watching Poppy for us.'

'Of course.' Cathy felt her blood rushing through her veins in hot waves as she wondered if this would be the real nanny.

Well, what could she expect? she told herself with a sinking feeling. It stood to reason that she couldn't get away with this for very much longer.

As soon as Pearce left her she got up and wandered around the room. She flicked idly through a pile of papers at one side of his desk. They were just normal household accounts. Her eyes moved quickly over the references Pearce had spread out over the desk—from an agency called Elite Nannies of London. Cathy pulled a face as her eyes moved down over it. Any moment now she would probably be confronted with an indignant Mabel Flowers and an absolutely furious Pearce Tyrone.

Frantically, she opened a couple of drawers in his desk but found only paper and discs. What she was looking for, she couldn't have said; she was just desperate for something…anything…she could use for her story before she was bodily thrown from the building.

She was in the process of closing the drawer when the telephone rang next to her. It rang and rang and Pearce didn't come to answer it.

Impulsively, Cathy snatched it up. 'Pearce Tyrone's residence,' she said in an efficient tone.

A woman with dulcet English tones asked to speak to Mr Tyrone.

'I'm afraid he isn't available at the moment,' Cathy said without hesitation. 'Can I take a message?'

There was the briefest pause before the woman asked to whom she was speaking.

'Mr Tyrone's secretary.' Cathy bit her lip. Well, it wasn't exactly a lie, she told herself. Tyrone had asked if she would do some typing for him.

'This is Janet Mercer of the Elite agency in London. I'm afraid the nanny we are sending you, a Ms Mabel Flowers, has run into some difficulty getting out to you. It's this French air-traffic control strike.'

Cathy's eyes widened; she could hardly believe her luck. 'We were wondering where she had got to.' She managed to sound slightly disapproving as she darted nervous glances towards the doorway in case Pearce should suddenly arrive.

'Yes, I know you wanted her right away and I did promise, but it's been chaotic trying to make other arrangements. The best we can do is book a train and the first available one is Monday next week, I'm afraid.'

'Dear me.' Cathy had difficulty keeping the glee from her voice.

'If you'd like to cancel our contract and get someone closer to home then we would understand.'

'No, leave it as it is,' Cathy told her nonchalantly. That would give her a week's grace to get her story, not that she intended to stay that long. She'd probably be out of here tomorrow morning with enough information to make Mike's year.

'Well, that's very good of you,' the woman said with evident relief.

Isn't it? Cathy thought, mentally patting herself on the back.

She was just putting down the phone when Pearce came back through the door.

'What are you doing?' he asked with a frown, noting her hand on the receiver and the fact that she was standing behind his desk.

'The phone rang.' Cathy hoped that her skin didn't look as hot as she felt. 'And, as you said you were short of a secretary, I dealt with it for you.'

'I'd rather you hadn't.' Pearce came further into the room and she sidled around the desk back to her own chair, feeling suitably chastised.

'I'm sorry, I was just trying to help.'

'Who was it?' He sat down and met her eyes. The directness, the unwavering way he seemed to look into her very soul, filled her with apprehension.

'Uh…they wouldn't say, actually.'

'Wouldn't say?' He barked the words with barely concealed impatience.

'Well—'

'Was it the hospital?' He leaned across towards her, his gaze searing.

Now she understood his irascible manner. He was worried about Jody Sterling, probably on tenterhooks waiting for news from the hospital.

'Oh, no,' she assured him swiftly, relaxing again. Then, thinking quickly, she added. 'Actually, I thought it might be a reporter. He was asking odd questions. Wanted to know if Jody Sterling's child was here and if you were the father of the child.'

The look of contemptuous disdain on Pearce Tyrone's face was awesome. Cathy shrank back in her chair as he made a very derisive statement about members of the press.

'What did you tell them?' He fixed her with a perishing glare.

'Nothing.' Cathy batted wide blue eyes at him. 'What should I have said?'

'You should have told them to mind their own damn business and that if they printed one word of a lie in their filthy rags I'd sue them from here to eternity.'

Pearce Tyrone was not a person to cross. She had

known it from the first moment she had set eyes on him.
His words now confirmed it even more. If she had any
sense she would get out of here p.d.q. This charade
would end in tears and they were most likely to be her
tears.

'Sorry.' Pearce leaned back in his chair and smiled
suddenly at her. 'I shouldn't be taking it out on you.'

'I...no...I'm sorry. I shouldn't have answered the
phone.' His smile did very strange things to her senses.

'Doesn't matter.' He waved a hand airily. 'Now,
where were we?'

Remembering the references for Mabel Flowers
spread before him, Cathy felt her apprehension growing.
'Actually, you were just about to pour me a black coffee,' she told him, an idea born of desperation forming
in her mind.

He turned and poured two cups, then handed one
across to her.

As she took it from him she moved awkwardly, and
pretended to lose her grip on the china saucer so that the
cup tipped down on the desk, spilling hot black liquid
all over the references.

'Oh, no... I'm so sorry.' Trying to sound horrified,
she picked up the crockery and watched the black stain
creep further over the papers.   Pearce said nothing, just
calmly reached for a box of tissues and started to mop
up the mess.

Cathy watched anxiously, hoping that she would at
least have succeeded in obliterating the name at the top
of the page.

'Not much damage done,' Pearce said easily.

'Here, let me help.' Cathy sprang to her feet and, taking a couple of tissues, she rubbed very hard at the top
of the page where the name was. She rubbed so hard
that the weakened paper tore.

Pearce's hand closed over hers. 'Ms Fielding.' His

voice took on a brusque edge. 'You are making matters worse.'

'Am I?' The touch of his hand against her skin was most disconcerting. She tried to ignore it and her hand closed in a tight fist, effectively scrunching up the tissue and taking the torn piece of the reference with it. Then she made to pull away from him.

He didn't release her and she looked at him, trying hard to keep her expression innocently questioning. Their faces seemed very close across the desk. She noticed that his eyes had darker flecks in them. His skin was smooth and healthily tanned. She could smell the faint, subtle tang of an expensive cologne. It was extremely pleasant, as was the whisper-soft feeling of his breath against her skin. Her nerve-endings seemed to prickle with consciousness.

'Is...is something wrong?' It took all her resources to keep her voice level.

His expression was hard and unyielding, just like the hand that held her. 'You've got a piece of the reference in your hand.'

'Have I? Oh, dear... I am sorry.' She fluttered her eyelashes. It was more a nervous reaction than a conscious effect.

Pearce's lips slanted in an unamused line. Very coolly and deliberately he uncurled her fingers and took the soggy paper from her.

She watched as he opened it and only when she saw that it was just a soggy mess did she relax slightly.

'I'm so sorry,' she muttered again, sitting back in her chair.

He regarded her steadily. 'I hope you are not normally so clumsy, Ms Fielding.' The censure in his tone was unmistakable.

'It was an accident. I did apologise.' A note of annoyance crept into her voice, but her anger was directed at herself. She felt guilty for this deceit...yet she felt compelled to keep it up. It was the dogged reporter in her, she supposed. The scent of a story holding her almost against her will.

He swept the wet pages to one side. 'This is ridiculous,' he muttered. 'I have work to get on with. I'll ask the agency to fax over new copies later.'

'Shall I get back to the nursery?' It would almost be a relief to get away from his presence for a moment. Every time she met his eyes she felt overwhelmed by him. She supposed it was her guilty conscience. She wasn't used to lying—it certainly didn't come naturally to her.

'Stay where you are,' he ordered in a clipped voice.

He pulled out a clean piece of paper and picked up a pen. He didn't write anything, just tapped the pen on the page from time to time.

'I might remind you,' he said sternly, 'that my standards are high. That is why I contacted the Elite Agency.'

'Of course.' She hoped that her demure tone didn't sound sarcastic.

'I told the Agency to send me no less than their best person.'

Cathy said nothing to that. She was too busy wondering what his requirements were. She didn't have to wonder long.

'The agency tell me you are a cordon bleu cook,' Pearce continued, watching her steadily.

Cathy tried not to blanch; she could barely boil an egg.

'As I stated in my telephone call to Mrs Roberts...uh, it is Mrs Roberts at the agency, is it not?'

Cathy hesitated and then ventured boldly, 'Well, actually, I have only ever dealt with Janet Mercer.' She felt rather pleased with herself as Pearce nodded.

'Oh, yes, I spoke to Mrs Mercer the first time I contacted the agency. I told her I wanted someone to run the house, cook, clean and take very good care of Poppy.' He reached for his coffee and took a sip.

Cathy noticed that he hadn't offered her a fresh cup. Probably afraid of what she would do with it.

'And, as I want you to do some typing for me in your spare time I think we should draw up a timetable and get organised.'

Cathy tried not to pull a face. She was very glad that she wouldn't be staying around here for too long. Cooking, cleaning, baby-minding...typing! Even Mary Poppins hadn't had it that hard.

'Would you like to say anything?' Pearce leaned back in his chair and regarded her steadily.

Something about his flint-like expression made her temper simmer. There were a few things she would have liked to say, but nothing would be gained from airing her views about him being a slave-driver. Wait until Mike heard about this, she thought grimly.

Instead she asked coolly, 'How much are you going to pay me?' Of course she had no intention of hanging around to be paid, but it might make interesting reading.

He frowned. 'Hasn't the agency told you?'

'Yes.' She shrugged, and tried to look nonchalant. 'But now you want me to do extra duties, such as typing.'

One eyebrow lifted. 'You are direct, Ms Fielding. A quality I admire.' He paused for just a moment. 'Let's round your salary up, then.'

He proceeded to name an amount that nearly made her fall off the chair. It was no wonder that Pearce expected a lot—he was paying a small fortune. Her theory about him being a slave-driver had been way off the mark; he was paying for a top service. 'Is that acceptable, Ms Fielding?'

'Yes, that's fine.' She tried to make her tone flat so that she didn't sound as stunned as she felt.

'And you can have Friday off.'

'Fine.' Again her voice was neutral. She wouldn't be here until Friday; she had no intention of lingering a moment longer than was necessary. 'But I do need to go into Antibes this evening,' she ventured. She needed to get back into town, phone her editor and collect some clothes from the hotel. 'I've...I've got an appointment and—'

'You waste no time. Hot date, is it?' Pearce's voice was dry.

'No...no.' Cathy shook her head vehemently, perhaps too vehemently because Pearce Tyrone was watching her with a look that could have cut glass at twenty paces.

'Ms Fielding, I asked for a nanny who could dedicate herself to Poppy for a while. The child needs good quality care to help her adjust to her new surroundings. I don't want or need a nanny who is panting with desire to escape into the arms of her lover every evening. If that is your calibre then you had better leave now.'

Cathy's mouth dropped. 'Panting with desire?' Her voice trembled with fury. 'How dare you speak to me like that?'

'Oh, I dare anything, Ms Fielding,' he assured her solemnly. 'My priority is Poppy. I need to know she is well looked after. So we may as well be up front about this. You will not go to Antibes tonight. If you feel you cannot dedicate your time exclusively to this baby and this house for the time I have hired you then you had better tell me now, and we needn't waste any more of each other's time.'

'You are also very direct, Mr Tyrone.' There was an edge of derision in her voice. 'Now I know why you admired the quality so much.'

'So, we understand each other?'

'Perfectly.'

'Good.' He drawled the word and leaned back into his chair again, a small smile of satisfaction playing around his strongly sensuous lips.

Her eyes moved over his strong profile thoughtfully, and she mentally penned what she might write about him. He was autocratic, with very little warmth, though fantastically good-looking, like a movie star.

She was very attracted to him. The thought flew in from nowhere and she tried to dismiss it. All women would be attracted to Pearce Tyrone—he had a kind of animal magnetism. It was a type of fatal attraction—at the same time as being drawn to him almost against your will, there was the fear that could just devour you.

'So...' Pearce drawled thoughtfully, jolting her back to reality. 'All that remains is for me to draw you up a timetable for tomorrow. You needn't bother with dinner tonight—coffee and a sandwich will do. I want to get on with my work.' Pearce scribbled on the paper as he spoke. 'But for tomorrow, let's see... For breakfast, I think, French toast and coffee.' He glanced up at her in that unnerving way of his. 'Breakfast, seven o'clock sharp. I like punctuality. I hope that's not a problem?'

'Not if it isn't with Poppy,' Cathy answered sweetly. Inside she was wondering if this guy was for real. And what the hell was French toast, anyway?

'Lunch at one sharp, something light; you can surprise me. I'm sure with your talents for cooking you can be quite imaginative.'

Oh, she could surprise him all right, Cathy thought grimly. And with a bit of luck she could give him heart-burn into the bargain.

As she listened to him her mind veered towards the article she was expected to write. It struck her that it might take her longer than she had first anticipated to get the necessary information. It was not going to be easy to break through Tyrone's businesslike reserve. She could hardly start asking pertinent questions when all he wanted to talk about was the daily running of the house. She needed to approach this cautiously.

She would have to get into town and phone Mike and pick up some of her belongings from the hotel. It was imperative.

She cleared her throat and cut across him. 'What about the shopping?' She asked the question in a wild attempt to get away from the house for a while. 'You haven't allowed me any time for getting ingredients for dinner and so on.'

'Don't worry about that. Henri will probably see to it...or we'll have whatever you need delivered.'

Silence stretched for a moment as she searched her mind for a way to get around him and out of here. 'Actually, I prefer to pick my own ingredients for cooking. I'm rather selective when shopping for dinner.'

'So is Henri.' Pearce was unmovable, his eyes firm.

'Yes, but I have to go into town tomorrow anyway... I need to collect the rest of my luggage,' she said as desperation started to creep in.

'Where is your luggage?' He leaned forward. 'I thought you just flew in from London early this morning?'

'Well, I... No...' She felt her skin go red and blotchy with discomfort as she searched around for a good excuse to explain why her clothes were in Antibes. Hell, she was no good at telling lies.

'There must be some misunderstanding, I have come straight from working for another family in Antibes... Their daughter is going away to school so they no longer need me.'

'So why leave your belongings in their house?' His voice was arid, his eyes watchful.

'Well, it's...' She shook her head, willing herself to

think quickly. 'It's a precaution.' She almost gasped the words in relief as the excuse came to her in a rush. 'I like to make sure everything is above board and suitable before I move into someone's house...especially when that someone is a single male.'

There wasn't a flicker of emotion in the cool blue eyes as they swept over her heated face. 'I see. Well, you have nothing to fear from me, Ms Fielding, I can assure you of that.'

Somehow his words sounded more like an insult than reassurance. OK, so she probably wasn't his type. Jody Sterling was exceptionally beautiful, as well as talented. But there was no need for him to sound quite so disdainful. She wasn't ugly. Her skin burned with bright, angry colour but she forced herself to hold his gaze. 'Well, that is a considerable relief.' She was pleased by the way she was able to match his cool tone. 'I wouldn't like there to be any misunderstanding.'

'Neither would I.' He fixed her with a level stare. 'I never fraternise on a personal level with my staff.'

She had to hand it to Pearce Tyrone, Cathy thought grimly. He got ten out of ten for being able to put her back up. 'Very commendable,' she said sugar-sweetly.

He smiled and for a moment amusement lurked in his blue eyes. What was so funny about being an insular snob? Cathy thought furiously. He wouldn't be laughing when he read the article she was going to write about him. The thought was enough to lighten her spirits.

'As it happens, I have to go into Antibes tomorrow so we may as well go together,' Pearce continued smoothly.

Cathy frowned, her moment of pleasure dissolving. How would she get her clothes from the hotel and phone Mike if Pearce insisted on tagging along? To top it all he was going to expect her to go directly to somebody's house and she didn't know a soul in Antibes. This was getting to be too complicated by far. 'But what about Poppy? I mean, we can hardly all—'

'We can take Poppy with us. We shouldn't be long.' Pearce glanced at his watch. 'Now, if you don't mind, I have work to do.'

'Yes, of course.' Cathy gritted her teeth.

'Perhaps you would put my supper on a tray and bring it in here for me?'

His tone was dismissive, as if he had taken all he could of inconsequential talk. She had a wild urge to say something flippant like, Yes sir, three bags full, sir. Instead, she bit her lip.

Her chance to be irreverent and glib would come later when she poured her story about the real Pearce Tyrone out onto paper. He was going to make a very interesting subject.

CHAPTER THREE

As Cathy came out of Pearce's study Henri was coming down the stairs with Poppy in his arms. 'I think it is time for Poppy to be fed now, *mademoiselle*,' he said as he handed the child across to her.

Talk about being left holding the baby, Cathy thought sardonically as she looked down at the child.

Poppy gave her a smile, her chubby cheeks dimpling in a cute way. She was wearing a hand-smocked dress and a pair of knitted booties, and she looked adorable. There was something about her that made Cathy's heart contract.

'Before I go home, *mademoiselle*, I must show you how to operate the security gates.' Henri beckoned for her to follow him.

He brought her into the kitchen. It was a large room with a farmhouse-style refectory table, oak cupboards and a gleaming terracotta tiled floor. At the far side there was a TV monitor which showed the front gates, illuminated by floodlit security lights.

'Just switch here and here.' Henri flicked the controls on a panel next to the screen and she saw the gates opening and closing. 'Always ask who is out there before admitting anyone. *Monsieur* only lets people in who have an appointment. He is a very busy man.'

'Yes, I understand.' She had been very lucky to get in here, she thought wryly.

'I shall go now and perhaps you will close the gates as I drive through?'

She nodded. 'I take it you don't live in?'

'No. I have a cottage a few miles away.'

Well, that was good news, Cathy thought happily. If Pearce was working in his study she could have a good look around the house later on without any interruptions.

She wondered if she dared to ring the newspaper from here.

Poppy moved fretfully in her arms. 'I had better feed this little one,' she said, smiling at Henri as she placed the child in a high chair by the table.

Henri turned and opened one of the kitchen cupboards. 'I think you will find everything you need for Poppy's meals in here,' he said.

Relief was overwhelming as she saw the jars of baby food and the packets with clearly written instructions. 'Thank you, Henri,' she said, her tone perhaps a little too heartfelt.

He nodded. 'I go now, *mademoiselle*. Do not forget to lock up after me.'

'I won't.' He was quite a kindly type of man, she decided. It was just a pity that he didn't seem inclined towards a bit of gossip. She decided to try again with him. 'So, what do you do around here, Henri?' she asked in a friendly tone.

'I look after the garden, clean the pool.' He shrugged. 'Just keep the residence in good order.'

'And do you find Monsieur Tyrone a good person to work for?'

Henri nodded. 'My wife and I have worked for him for over twelve years.' He paused then, a look of sadness on his face. 'My wife, Sophie, died five months ago.' There was a wealth of sorrow in the older man's voice and Cathy immediately felt sad for him. 'I'm so sorry,' she told him sincerely.

He patted her shoulder as he saw the genuine sympathy on her face. 'We had thirty years of marriage and I have a lot of good memories. Now I have my grandchildren and my job…. Monsieur Tyrone has been very understanding.' He paused for just a moment, before saying, 'But, then, the *Monsieur* knows what it is like to love someone and lose them.'

'Does he?' Before Cathy could ask about this Henri cut across her, his manner suddenly agitated. 'I am talking too much.' He moved away towards the door. 'Don't forget to close the gates when I have gone.'

Cathy watched him leave with a feeling of acute disappointment. Just a few more moments and she could have learnt so much more. To whom had he been referring? Whom had Pearce loved and lost?

The sound of Poppy crying cut across her thoughts and she turned to see to the child.

By the time Cathy brought Pearce's supper in to him on a tray she was starting to feel tired. She hadn't had a spare moment to look around the house—her time had been completely taken up with Poppy.

Looking after a baby was very hard work, but she had surprised herself by handling it quite well. In fact, there was a part of her that had enjoyed the experience. Poppy was a lovable child.

Pearce barely looked up as she came in. He was sitting in front of the computer terminal, his hands busy on the keyboard.

Cathy put the tray on the table next to him.

'How is Poppy?'

Without being invited, she sat down on the chair opposite him. 'Asleep at last. She took a while to settle.'

Pearce looked up, an expression of concern on his handsome features. 'Do you think it is because she is in unfamiliar surroundings?'

Cathy shrugged. 'If she was a bit older I'd say she was missing her mother. Is there any news about Ms Sterling's condition yet?'

He shook his head. 'I rang earlier; there is no change.'

He sounded worried and Cathy's heart went out to him. It was a dreadful situation. 'Poor little Poppy,' she said softly.

Pearce looked over at her and his lips slanted in a half-smile. 'I noticed that you and Poppy were having quite a conversation in the kitchen earlier.'

She felt her skin flare with colour. While she had been spoon-feeding Poppy her dinner she had been talking to her, trying to encourage her to eat up. She recalled now that she had got quite carried away, talking in a singsong gentle way in babyish rubbish.

'I put my head around the door, just to see how you were getting on,' he said in answer to her questioning look.

'I didn't see you.' Her skin felt as if it were on fire. He must have thought she was completely daft.

'No, you were absorbed with Poppy, so much so that I didn't like to disturb you.'

She had been absorbed. She had felt a deep tenderness for the little girl. The power of the feeling had taken her by surprise. She wondered if it was because she had lost her own mother when she'd been just a baby. Whether, deep down in her subconscious, this was why she felt such empathy for the child.

'Don't look so embarrassed,' Pearce said. 'You don't know what a relief it was to see you acting so naturally with Poppy, so gently. She is going to need a lot of extra love and attention to help her through this period.'

His sensitivity and concern for Poppy touched her. So much so that she found herself saying nothing, just staring at him and taking in everything about him—the way his dark hair gleamed like midnight under the overhead light, the chiselled strength of his features.

He returned her gaze. For just the briefest interlude there was a silence, tinged with some kind of emotion that Cathy couldn't quite define.

She was the first to look away. She was supposed to be asking him questions, concentrating on her story. She shook her head, trying to dispel the warm fog that had invaded her brain like cotton wool.

'I'm sure you are right.' Her voice became brisk, businesslike. 'So, tell me, are you working on a new book?' Abruptly she switched the subject to something less emotive.

His expression altered, became harder. 'Yes.'

From the bluntness of the reply she took it that now they were no longer discussing Poppy Pearce was now waiting for her to leave him in peace. She could sense the sudden tension in him, feel his impatience. But despite this, or maybe because of this, she deliberately lingered. Her eyes moved around the room and lighted on a shelf that was filled with his books.

'You've been very prolific, haven't you?' She got to her feet and wandered over to have a closer look. She noticed his latest book, *Theory of Murder*, and took it out. 'I haven't read this,' she murmured, her eyes scanning the blurb on the back. 'They've turned it into a film, haven't they?'

He nodded. 'Take it, if you want,' he offered casually, perhaps in an endeavour to be rid of her quickly.

'Thanks.' She smiled at him, but made no attempt to leave. 'I have a confession to make—I have only read a few of your books.'

'Murder stories and political thrillers aren't everyone's idea of an entertaining read.'

'Oh, I did enjoy them,' Cathy told him sincerely. 'It's just that I don't get much time for reading, so I tend to choose light novels.'

'Let me guess…romance?'

She shrugged. 'Yes, I like romantic fiction. *Pride and Prejudice* is one of my favourite books.' She fixed him with a direct look. 'You don't seem to put much romance in your stories... Why is that?'

It was a question she would have asked had she been interviewing him and she waited, feeling pleased that she had managed to inject it in so easily.

'Love is a powerful emotion. I do use it occasionally. Clarissa, for instance, in, *Hell Hath no Fury* was driven by desire. It blinded her; it changed her from an ordinary woman into a cold-blooded killer.'

'Yes, I read that book.' She shivered as she remembered it. 'I found it quite terrifying. Your hero, there was no love interest for him—'

'He had a few flings.' For just a moment Pearce looked amused.

'Yes, I know there is sex in the book.' Cathy felt herself colouring up, for some reason feeling suddenly embarrassed. 'But that's hardly the same thing, is it?'

'Isn't it?' There was definite amusement in his blue eyes now and she felt her composure slipping.

'Well, he doesn't fall in love with anyone...there's no happy ending for him.'

The brief moment of amusement faded. 'No, but that is life sometimes.'

Cathy remembered how Henri had told her that Pearce had loved and lost somebody. 'That's rather a sad statement,' she said gently.

One eyebrow lifted. 'Is it? I think it is a realistic statement.'

'Basically what you are saying is that you are not a romantic?'

'I'm a writer, Ms Fielding, and I enjoy my work...when I'm allowed to get on with it.'

She knew that he wanted her to leave but she was loath to go. She batted wide beautiful eyes. 'Am I disturbing you?' Something made her lower her voice to a soft husky tone. Why she spoke like that she didn't

know; it was some kind of feminine instinct that just
seemed to take over.

For a moment his eyes moved downwards to the soft
curves of her body. The movement caused a quiver of
awareness to steal over her from absolutely nowhere. 'In
a word…yes.'

The sound of the telephone cut the sudden tense silence that fell between them.

Pearce snatched up the receiver immediately, a frown
etched very clearly on his handsome features.

Cathy stood where she was, unashamedly watching
him. Obviously it wasn't the hospital because he relaxed
immediately on hearing whoever was at the other end of
the line.

'No, John, there is no news yet. I rang the hospital a
little while ago and her condition is unchanged.' He
raked a hand in a distracted way through his hair. 'I
know…it's terrible, and to add to everything we've got
a damn air strike. I had planned to fly up every day to
see Jody…now I don't know what to do. It's a long drive
and I've got Poppy to consider…'

Pearce flicked a glance up at Cathy, then covered the
mouthpiece. 'Haven't you got work to do?' he asked her
curtly.

'Yes, of course.' She moved towards the door very
slowly so that she could hear as much of his conversation as possible.

'Poppy is fine. I've got—' He covered the mouthpiece
of the phone with his hand for just a moment and his
voice boomed over towards her. 'Ms Fielding, please
pick up your feet and leave.'

Pearce Tyrone certainly didn't waste time trying to be
polite, she thought wryly. She cringed as she remembered the flirtatious way she had spoken to him a moment ago.

She shook her head, wondering what on earth she had

been thinking of. Trying to flirt with Tyrone was like trying to play with a panther. She must never ever do that again, she told herself crossly.

She closed the door behind her and went upstairs.

She was no sooner in the nursery door than Poppy started to cry.

'What's the matter, sweetheart?' Cathy leaned over the cot. The child looked hot, her cheeks were flushed and she cried fretfully. Cathy put a soothing hand to her forehead and was relieved to find she didn't have a temperature. Gently, she reached in and picked her up.

'Let's change you into something a little cooler and check your nappy,' she murmured as she put the baby down on a changing mat on the floor.

Poppy stopped crying as soon as Cathy took off her nappy. It didn't need changing but she decided to put on a fresh one anyway.

Poppy seemed to like the cool freedom of being without it because she kicked her legs in vigorous delight.

Poor little mite, Cathy thought as she watched her. She hoped and prayed that Jody Sterling would make a complete recovery. She stroked a stray curl from the little girl's face. At least Poppy had a caring father. She had very little doubt that Pearce was Poppy's father. Why else would the child be here?

'You like being without that nappy, don't you?' Cathy said in a gentle voice. 'Yes, you do.'

What was it about babies that made you talk in that ridiculous tone? Cathy wondered with a wry smile as she lifted the child and gently patted her dry with a towel before reaching for some cream and some talc. Even so, it was quite fun—like going back to a second childhood, she told herself as she hummed a little song to Poppy. Not the same kind of fun as lying in the sun with a gin and tonic...but it was engagingly rewarding.

You didn't feel self-conscious, acting silly with a

baby—it was like letting all your inhibitions down and just being yourself.

She turned the talc container upside down to lightly dust the child's skin. Unfortunately she didn't realise how fast the talc would come out and white powder flew everywhere.

'Oh, wonderful,' Cathy remarked drily as she surveyed the chalk-white little legs. 'Just wonderful.'

Poppy gurgled happily, as if sharing the joke. 'Well might you laugh at me—'

'Everything all right, Ms Fielding? Pearce Tyrone's curt tone interrupted the proceedings abruptly.

Cathy looked around, dismayed to be caught in such a mess. She was sitting in the middle of the floor, Poppy's things spread around her like a bring-and-buy sale and talc everywhere. A man like Pearce Tyrone would not be amused.

'Yes, fine, thank you.'

'I though I heard Poppy crying.'

'She was a little hot, that's all. I'm just going to put her in a cool cotton vest.' As she spoke she dusted the child down lightly with a towel and then reached for a new nappy.   She had hoped that Pearce would go. She felt nervous with him watching her. However, instead of leaving he came further into the room to stand over her.

She pulled open the sticky tapes on the disposable nappy and pressed them down into place but infuriatingly they sprang open again.

Poppy kicked her dimpled, chubby legs in delight as once more she felt herself free.

Acutely aware of Pearce watching her, Cathy tried again but still the nappy wouldn't fasten.

'You've got cream on the sticky tape,' Pearce remarked calmly. The next moment he was kneeling beside her.

'Come here, little honey.' He pulled the changing mat

closer to him and took another fresh nappy from the pack.

Cathy watched with a mixture of annoyance and admiration as the nappy went on perfectly for him.

'There, nothing to it.' He sat back on his heels and grinned at Cathy.

'I was managing perfectly until you came along,' she told him primly.

'Yes...so I noticed.' He smiled at her, his eyes moving over her features with a kind of absorbed fascination. The way he was looking at her made her heart beat crazily against her ribs.

He was sitting very close to her, she realised suddenly, and there was a warmth in his eyes that really threw her.

'You've got talc on your nose,' he said, a humorous note in his voice.

'Oh!' Embarrassment swept through her. She had thought that he was looking at her admiringly and instead of that he had probably been thinking that she looked an utter mess.

Before she could lift up a hand to rub the offending talc away he reached out and did it for her. The touch of his hand against her skin sent a shooting sensation through her.

'There, that's better. You've got a very pretty nose.' The dark blue eyes swept over her again, then seemed to linger on the soft curves of her lips.

She felt a dizziness inside her that she had never felt before.

'A pretty face, too,' he murmured, and for just a moment all hint of humour was missing from his expression and he was studying her very seriously.

For a second she thought he was going to say something else...something deeper.

Cathy moistened her lips. She didn't understand the tension that had suddenly sprung up between them. It was thrilling... It was ludicrous... She was here to get a story, she told herself staunchly; she couldn't feel any kind of attraction for him...it wasn't right.

He was the one to move away from her, a shuttered expression going down across his handsome face. 'Well, I suppose we should see if we can get this little lady settled back in her cot.'

Cathy nodded and stood up. 'I'll get that vest for her.' Desperately she tried to sound light-hearted and normal, but to her own ears her voice sounded strained.

She noticed the warmth in his eyes as he looked at Poppy and the gentle way he picked her up and held her as Cathy put the baby's nightwear on.

'She seems more settled now,' Cathy remarked as he laid Poppy down tenderly in the cot and reached to brush a feather-light kiss on her forehead.

The child did look sleepy now. It was obvious that she was fighting to keep her eyes open.

'God, I hope Jody's going to be all right,' Pearce said suddenly, a wealth of sadness in his eyes as he watched the child.

Cathy's heart constricted painfully. 'You and I both. That little girl is going to need her mother.'

Pearce looked over at her, then he smiled gently. 'Sometimes, Catharine Fielding,' he said lightly, 'I think you are a nice person.'

She felt her skin flush with colour. 'There's no need to sound so surprised.' She managed to inject a glint of humour into her voice. 'I *am* a nice person.'

He smiled and, with a last glance at Poppy, he walked toward the door. 'I'll be in my study if you need anything.'

The return to a businesslike tone made her wonder if she had imagined the earlier look in his eyes...the atmosphere that had suddenly flared between them.

For a long time after he had gone she stood watching

Poppy as she slept, her mind going over and over the way he had talked to her—the way he had looked at her.

She had imagined the warmth in his eyes, she told herself fiercely. Pearce was in love with Jody Sterling. It was obvious that he was worried sick about her.

She raked a hand through her hair and was even more annoyed to find that she was trembling with reaction.

She was here to get a story, she told herself fiercely over and over again. She couldn't let anything else cloud her mind.

She took a deep breath. Before Poppy had started to cry she had planned to take some more photographs of the house while everything was quiet.

To prove to herself that she still had this assignment under control—that her judgement wasn't starting to be emotionally coloured—she turned away from the cot and went to get her camera from the wardrobe. She would carry on and do her job.

Her heart thudded nervously as she opened different doors along the landing. Most were spare rooms, beautiful but devoid of personal possessions. It wasn't until she came back and opened the door opposite to the nursery that she found what had to be Pearce Tyrone's bedroom.

It was austerely masculine, dominated by a huge bed. Dark wood and dark blues complemented the modern paintings on the wall. A suit was hung casually over a clothes press. A few gold-framed photographs sat on the bedside table.

With a feeling of trepidation, Cathy took out her camera and pushed the door further open.

She aimed at the bed and clicked then, closing the door behind her, she walked further in to have a closer look at the photographs.

One was of a newborn baby, the other of a young, attractive blonde. Cathy picked up the one of the young woman, trying to decide if it was Jody Sterling or not. She was fairly certain that it was but it was hard to tell. Jody was one of those chameleon-like people who could look totally different every time you looked at her.

She photographed the bedside table, then turned to leave the room.

She had just put her camera safely away in the nursery again when the gate bell sounded loudly through the house.

Cathy glanced anxiously at Poppy to see if the noise had disturbed her, but the child was fast asleep. Her little face looked less flushed now and she seemed more peaceful. Cathy pulled the blanket up around her again and watched the steady rise and fall of her breathing, making sure that she was all right before she went to see who was outside.

Pearce had already opened the front door and Cathy paused in the shadows at the top of the stairs to watch quietly.

The front of the house was lit up as the automatic security lights went on, highlighting the red sports car which stopped by the front door.

A woman in her early thirties came up to the front door. She was tall and attractive with dark shining hair which swung in a well-cut bob and she was wearing a navy blue short-sleeved trouser suit.

'Laura, this is a lovely surprise. I thought you were jetting off to New York today.'

'Well, darling, I would have been, except for this air-traffic control strike.' She reached up to kiss him. Cathy couldn't make out if she kissed him on the cheek or on the lips, although she strained her eyes.

'Any news about Jody yet?'

'No, none.' Pearce's voice was heavy.

'And how's Poppy? Was the drive down from Paris with her awful?'

'No, not too bad, actually. It was when we got here that I started to have problems with her. She just wouldn't stop crying.' He put an arm across her shoulder. 'Come on into the lounge and have a drink and I'll tell you all about it.'

As they turned Pearce looked directly towards the stairs. 'Everything all right, Ms Fielding?' he asked nonchalantly.

Startled, Cathy took a moment to answer. She stepped out of the shadows and tried to look as if she was just on her way downstairs and not eavesdropping. 'Yes, everything's fine, Mr Tyrone,' she said primly.

He smiled and she had the distinct impression that he knew very well that she had been listening. 'Perhaps you would be good enough to make Ms Houston and me a pot of coffee?'

'Yes, of course.'

The lounge door closed behind them.

When Cathy brought through a tray of coffee a little while later Laura was curled up on one of the leather settees with her shoes off.

Pearce was standing by the marble fireplace, a glass of brandy in his hand. He was saying something to the woman which was causing her great amusement. Her head was thrown back, showing the milky-white length of her smooth neck and the low cut of her blouse.

For some reason Cathy felt a stab of annoyance at the intimacy of the moment. Why, she couldn't have said.

'Thank you.' Pearce came across and took the heavy tray from her. 'Laura Houston, meet Poppy's nanny, Catherine Fielding. I wouldn't have managed to get through this afternoon without her.'

'Really?' Laura had very dark probing eyes and they did a comprehensive sweep over Cathy. 'You don't look like a nanny.'

'What are nannies supposed to look like?' Cathy replied, instantly antagonised by the patronising tone.

'Well…' Laura shook her head. 'You're right, it was a silly thing to say. It's just that you are really quite pretty.'

Cathy gritted her teeth. She had met lots of very beautiful girls when she had been interviewing nannies for her article on child care. 'Thank you, so are you,' she retorted in exactly the same condescending tone.

She met Pearce's eyes across the room and felt disconcerted when she saw the gleam of humour on his face.

'Laura is my agent,' he told her. 'We do a lot of work together.'

Suddenly Cathy realised just who this woman was. Laura Houston was an agent for a host of successful writers and she was a power to be reckoned with in the world of publishing.

'You make me sound boring, darling… We do have some fun…sometimes, don't we?'

'Sometimes we have a dinner or two.' There was a patient note in Pearce's voice, as if he was used to this flirtatious kind of talk from Laura and not really impressed by it.

But, then, Pearce was probably used to lots of women flirting with him, Cathy thought as she remembered that she had fallen victim to that particular sin earlier. The memory made her cringe.

Laura took the coffee that Pearce handed her and seemed unruffled by his cool reply. 'So, darling, now that I'm forced to stay on at my villa for a while longer I've decided to throw a party and invite absolutely everyone. The invitation is for tomorrow night, eight o'clock.'

Cathy took her time walking towards the door, so that she could hear his reply.

'I can't, Laura.' Pearce's voice was firm. 'For one thing I'm not in the mood for parties, and for another I have Poppy to consider.'

'A party is what you need.' Laura said firmly. She sounded a little annoyed. 'And you've got a nanny for Poppy.'

'I don't want to leave her, Laura. Poppy is very precious to me; please try to understand.' There was no prevarication in the tone. Pearce wasn't about to be swayed on the subject, that was for sure.

Cathy looked back across the room at him, her hand on the doorhandle. She liked him tremendously at that moment. In fact, the strength of her feeling was so strong that it was almost overwhelming.

Pearce glanced over and caught her staring at him. As soon as their eyes met she felt the same as she had earlier in the nursery. The attraction was intense.

'Goodnight.' She forced herself to smile politely, yet her heart was thumping in a very strange way.

CHAPTER FOUR

DESPITE the fact that Cathy was practically naked beneath the crisp linen sheets she was unbearably hot. She felt very tired and yet unable to sleep. The house was quiet, its deep, dark silence somehow unnerving.

She thought again about how she had felt about Pearce tonight. She had rationalised her feelings and she understood them. She had felt drawn to Pearce because he was a good father. But understanding didn't make the emotionalism go away.

She admired the way Pearce put his daughter first, possibly because her own father had found that so difficult to do. He had practically left Cathy's upbringing in the hands of her elder sister, Eva. Poor Eva had been just sixteen, very young to have the responsibility of a young child thrust upon her. But she had coped admirably well. Cathy was still very grateful for all that her sister had done for her.

She threw off the sheets and stared at the luminous face of the clock on her bedside table. It was nearly three in the morning. If she was going to lie awake she should be thinking about the article she had to write about Pearce, not dwelling on the emotional issues.

Laura Houston had left soon after her coffee. Cathy had heard her at the doorway, trying once more to persuade Pearce to come to her party.

She smiled now as she remembered Pearce's cool reply. He obviously wasn't a man who could be easily flattered or coerced. She liked that about him. She liked the way he talked about Poppy…the protective light in his eyes.

She got out of bed and opened the window to let in some air. It was a little fresher outside, but not much. She leaned on the window-ledge. The moon was almost full in the soft velvet of the sky. She could hear the gentle sound of the Mediterranean lapping against the shore and the constant hum of the cicadas. It was a tranquil, almost exotic sound. London and her hectic life at the paper seemed like another planet away.

There were moments, and this was one of them, when Cathy wondered what it would be like to give up her job and flee to tropical climes. But, then, as her sister was fond of telling her, in a rather belligerent way, she was married to her career.

Eva was always trying to get her married off, introducing her to 'eligible men' as she called them.

There had been a special man in Cathy's life once. David Collins was a freelance photographic journalist and they had met on assignment in Singapore. David had been charming and Cathy had thought herself deeply in love. Getting engaged to him had been a terrible mistake and the affair had ended badly.

Now Cathy didn't want deep involvement. She didn't want to need anyone...she didn't want to depend on someone else for her happiness. As far as she could see—with just a few rare exceptions—generally, and on the whole, men let you down. Better to be self-sufficient.

The sound of the baby crying broke the silence of the house. With complete disregard for the fact that she was only wearing a lacy pair of panties and a silk camisole, Cathy dashed across into the other room. 'What is it, darling?' she cooed as she looked down into the cot.

Poppy stared up at her with wide, tearful eyes.

'Come on, then.' Cathy bent to pick her up.

'I don't know a lot about babies, but I do know you shouldn't pick them up every time they cry.'

The voice came from behind her, sending a wave of

horror and embarrassment washing through her. Pearce
had no right to just waltz in here when the mood suited
him. She was practically nude, for heaven's sake! The
camisole she was wearing was so fine that it was almost
transparent.

For a second she just stood there, unsure which way
to move or what to say. Should she turn around and hold
Poppy against her as a cover, or keep her back firmly
towards him? Her eyes caught on the cover in Poppy's
cot and she caught it up swiftly in one hand, draped it
over the child and picked both up, effectively screening
herself as she turned.

'How dare you come into my bedroom like this?' she
blazed furiously.

He was leaning indolently against the doorframe, still
fully dressed. 'This isn't your room,' he said, unperturbed. 'Your room is through there.' He nodded towards
the connecting bedroom.

'Well, you still have no right to just barge in here at
this hour of the night.' She burned with embarrassment
and indignation as his gaze moved slowly up over the
long bare length of her legs, the soft curve of her hips
and her narrow waist. She clutched the child's blanket
nervously at her breast, hoping that it adequately covered
her.

'Well, you have no right to walk around the house
like that,' he drawled.

'I'm not walking around the house, I'm in the nursery,' Cathy corrected sharply. 'Are you accusing me of
being deliberately provocative?'

'Do you usually walk around the nursery half naked?'
he asked, transferring his attention to her heated face and
the soft fall of her long honey-blonde hair. 'Because if
so I'm not surprised you've had problems with previous
male employers.'

'I've...I've never had problems with any employers,'

she denied forcefully, her heart racing. That he should think that she was deliberately flaunting herself was preposterous. She was walking around like this because she hadn't got any nightwear with her, but no matter how she was dressed he shouldn't be in here.

'I rather gained the impression that you had,' he remarked. 'Your reticence to move in here completely until you had fully checked me out led me to assume—'

'You assume too much, Mr Tyrone,' she told him shakily. 'For your information, I have forgotten my night things. But if I had known you were going to walk in here in the middle of the night then I would have brought a suit of armour plating to wear, I can assure you. Now, if you don't mind, I would like you to leave so that I can attend to my charge.'

His lips slanted in a look of total amusement. Then, to her surprise, he turned around and left the room.

Cathy glanced down at Poppy. She had stopped crying but she was murmuring discontentedly. Her cheeks looked very red. Cathy put a hand on one and was shocked to feel how hot it was.

It was a welcome relief when Pearce returned to the nursery a moment later. 'Here, for the sake of my blood pressure—as well as your own—you had better put this on.' He held out a towelling robe.

'Thanks.' She made no move to take the dressing-gown from him. Her embarrassment and annoyance had melted into anxiety for Poppy. 'I'm a bit concerned about Poppy,' she said, looking down at the child with a frown. 'She seems to be burning up.'

Pearce came closer and put a hand on the child's forehead. 'She is very hot.'

'What do you think it is?' Cathy was past caring whether she sounded like a professional nanny. Her concern was all for Poppy.

'I don't know but we will soon find out. Give her to me and you put on this dressing gown.'

The brisk, efficient tone was reassuring. Cathy nodded, then hesitated as she realised that as soon as she relinquished Poppy she would be revealing far more that she wanted to.

'I'll close my eyes,' he told her drily as he saw the look of consternation cross her face.

'Thanks.' Swiftly she took the dressing-gown and then placed the baby in Pearce's arms.

He turned with Poppy as Cathy wrapped herself in the voluminous robe. It was obviously his—she could even smell the faint aroma of his cologne on it. There was something comforting about the feel of it next to her skin.

Cathy watched as Pearce checked Poppy's nappy. She was perfectly dry and clean.

'So, what is the matter, little one?' Cathy asked the baby soothingly as she started to cry again. She put her hand on Poppy's face, feeling the heat that was emanating from her.

The child turned her head and pushed dimpled little hands against her mouth, chewing on her fingers in a distressed way.

'Teething!' Both Pearce and Cathy spoke at the same time as the thought occurred to them simultaneously. Then they smiled at each other in pleased relief.

'I think we have got some soothing gel in the cupboard,' Cathy said as she hurried to open up the wardrobe at the far side of the room. 'I saw it earlier when I was....' She stopped herself from saying taking photographs and substituted, 'familiarising myself with the place', her tongue tripping over the words nervously. It would be so easy to make one mistake and then it would be all over.

She found the gel and turned to find Pearce watching her, a look of deep contemplation on his face.

'Here we are.' She forced a bright note into her voice. She was sure that Pearce hadn't noticed the slight hesitation in her speech, and even if he had, he couldn't possibly have a clue as to what she had very nearly said. Even so, he was watching her very closely. Maybe he thought it was strange that she hadn't realised straight away that Poppy was teething.

Poppy started to cry in earnest again and Pearce rocked her soothingly in his arms, then held her steady as Cathy put a little of the gel onto her fingers to apply it.

Poppy's gums were hot and she could feel the sharp underlying teeth at certain places, as if they were just waiting to burst through.

'Poor little thing—it must be agony,' Cathy said sympathetically as she put the top on the gel again.

The baby had stopped crying now, but she gave a little whimper as if to agree with her.

Cathy looked up and found that she was standing very close to Pearce. She could see the dark shadow along his jaw line and the dark flecks in the blue eyes. He looked tired, she thought suddenly, and it was very late for him to be still fully dressed.

'Have you just finished working?' she asked softly.

He nodded. 'I thought if I got as much as possible done while Poppy was asleep I could spend more time with her during the day.'

'You shouldn't overdo it. If you give Poppy to me I'll try to settle her back down for the night. There is no point in both of us losing sleep.'

'My sentiments exactly,' he said with a smile. 'So you go back to bed and I'll settle Poppy.'

She frowned. 'But it's my job to see to Poppy.' Even as she spoke she wondered if the role of nanny was going to her head. She was here to get a story, not stay up all night with a baby. Yet she was reluctant to leave the nursery.

His eyes moved over her face, noting the gentle concern in her wide eyes. 'You are good with children,' he said suddenly. 'I'm surprised you aren't married with a baby of your own.'

The remark took her by surprise, and she replied candidly, 'Well, I've never met anyone I loved well enough to marry.'

One eyebrow lifted as if he found that hard to believe.

'It is true.' Cathy's eyes moved to Poppy. The child was starting to look sleepy, her eyelids drooping. She looked sweet and angelic, rosy-cheeked with a curl that fell just in the centre of her forehead. 'I had a near miss once, though. Got engaged, then discovered just in time that it would have been a ghastly mistake.'

'Why would it have been a mistake?'

Cathy looked back up at him. 'Because he didn't love me... We had very little in common, really.' Her glance flicked back to Poppy. 'He didn't even like children and I wanted a family.'

Disconcerted at having made such a personal statement, she suddenly pulled herself up. 'Oh, it's a boring subject.' She wondered why she had told him that. She hadn't talked about David in a long, long time.

'I didn't find it boring.' His voice was gentle, encouraging.

She stepped back from him. 'Must be something about the small hours of the morning that makes for maudlin conversation.'

He smiled, a teasing light in his eyes. 'The hours before dawn are a good time for secrets.'

'Can I ask you something, then?' She spoke impulsively.

'Fire away, but that doesn't mean I'm going to answer.'

'Henri mentioned something today about you losing someone you loved. To whom was he referring?'

'Well, my father died a few years ago.' Pearce turned away from her as Poppy gave a small murmur. He rocked the child soothingly in his arms. Then his glance moved towards the window—to the darkness of the night. He was silent for just a moment, his forehead creased by a frown. 'But I presume Henri was referring to my wife.'

'I didn't know you had been married.' Cathy was stunned and it showed clearly in her voice.

He turned and looked at her. 'It was a long time ago. Long before my writing career.'

'So, what happened?' Even as she asked the question Cathy knew that her interest wasn't strictly professional.

His hesitation was momentary. 'Sarah and I were both qualified marine biologists. We met on a remote island in the South China Seas called Sujal.' His voice held a distant note, as if he wasn't really concentrating on what he was saying—as if he was somewhere else in his mind.

'We had both been sent by our respective companies to study a rare type of plankton, peculiar to the very deep waters off the island. Sujal was a magical place—volcanic, lush, completely unspoilt.' His lips twisted and there was a look of pain in his eyes as he said, 'And Sarah was the most beautiful woman. Very natural, honest, fun. I fell in love with her almost at first sight, and we got married out there by special licence.'

'Sounds very romantic.' Cathy could feel a dryness in her throat; her voice sounded husky and low.

'It was, and we had six weeks of wedded bliss. Then came the accident. Sarah had a problem with her diving equipment; she was very far down on the sea bed.' He shrugged, a helpless look on his face. 'They didn't get her up in time.'

'Were you there when it happened?'

He shook his head. 'I was on a flight to Australia, a two-day sojourn to file in reports for head office. Sarah was dead when I got back. I often think that if I had been with her maybe...' His voice trailed off and he shook his head. Then he looked at her directly. 'Maybe you are right. Something about the small hours of the morning does lead to melancholy. I haven't talked about Sarah for years.'

'Perhaps you need to,' Cathy said gently. 'They say it helps.'

He frowned and looked at her, his eyes changing and becoming hard. 'I somehow don't think it would help. For one thing, I hardly know you, do I?'

'And for another you never fraternise with your members of staff?' she asked with a raised eyebrow. The question was light-hearted but inside her duplicity weighed heavily.

He smiled. 'Perhaps we should forget about that?' Suddenly the atmosphere became charged again, filled with an emotion that made Cathy's heart thud unevenly.

'Perhaps I had better turn in for the night.' Cathy was the one to look away. She glanced at Poppy, who was now fast asleep in Pearce's arms, before she turned towards her bedroom door. 'Goodnight, Pearce.' She didn't realise that she had used his first name until he used hers.

'Goodnight, Catherine,' he said quietly.

She didn't get into bed again straight away but sat on the edge, holding Pearce's robe tightly around her body. Beside her on the bedside table there was the pen and paper with which she had tried to jot down a few notes about Pearce earlier. She had lots to add to it now.

Pearce's brief marriage would be a revelation to everyone.

She glanced at the paper but didn't pick it up. Instead she got back into bed and turned over. For no apparent reason, the thing that stuck forcibly in her mind was that one of the factors Pearce had given for loving his wife was her honesty.

CHAPTER FIVE

MONDAY morning had never looked like this, or felt like this, in London, Cathy thought as she leaned against the kitchen sink and stared dreamily out of the window.

Back home her desk at the paper would be chaotic, the phone ringing, and the computers blinking accusingly at her.

Sunshine glimmered over the swimming pool, and in the distance the mountains looked purple against the brilliant blue wash of the sky.

Henri was planting some shrubs in the colourful borders beside the table and chairs on the patio. He lifted his hand in a salute as he noticed her watching him.

There was a warmth in the air, a vibrance of colour and tranquillity that made Cathy feel unaccountably content.

Poppy gurgled happily in her high chair and tapped her empty bottle against her table in a series of small thuds.

'Come on, darling, don't do that.' Cathy moved to take it from her.

As she turned, her eyes lighted on the telephone on the wall. The sight of it was like a recrimination. She knew that Mike would be waiting for her to contact him. He would want to know what she had found out. She took a deep breath. She didn't dare ring from here, she told herself staunchly. It was too risky.

Pearce appeared in the doorway. He was wearing fawn-coloured trousers and a soft cream shirt. Despite his late night last night, he looked remarkably fresh.

'Good morning.' He ruffled the top of Poppy's head

with an affectionate hand as he passed by her to take a seat at the table. 'And how are you today?'

'Poppy is fine.' Cathy put a fresh pot of coffee on the table and smiled at him. 'She has eaten all her breakfast and seems to be in much better humour.'

'Well, that's good news.' His eyes moved from the child to her, sweeping over her appearance and making her wish that she was wearing something different from the plain white dress of yesterday.

'And how about you? Are you tired after our late night?'

The words sounded intimate to Cathy. 'No, I'm fully recovered.' She tucked a stray strand of blonde hair behind her ear and tried to make herself think businesslike thoughts. Pearce was being polite, nothing more, and Poppy had kept them up very late last night. 'I'll make you some breakfast,' she offered, then glanced around at the work counters. 'I've put that list you gave me yesterday down somewhere—'

'Don't bother for me, Catherine. I just want coffee this morning.' He indicated the chair opposite to him. 'Why don't you relax and join me?'

She sat down and watched as he poured them both coffee. 'Has Henri had a drink?' he enquired before putting down the pot.

She nodded. 'I took him one out earlier.'

It felt cosy, sitting at the breakfast table with Pearce and Poppy. It was as if she was part of a family. The thought made her cheeks flare with colour. She was here to spy on him and report back to her paper. Guilt murmured it's incommodious way through her.

'I thought Laura Houston seemed very nice,' she remarked idly, trying to prove to herself that her first priority was her article for the paper. All she needed was a little more background on the women in Pearce's life and how Jody Sterling fitted in and then she could be out of here.

'Did you?' He sounded disinterested.

'Yes. Have you known her long?'

'Years. She is my agent. She has a villa not far from me here, and we are also neighbours in London. So I do tend to see a lot of her.'

The shrill ring of the phone interrupted them and Pearce stood up to answer it.

For a while the conversation was one-sided, then Pearce said, 'That's wonderful news' The relief in his voice was very evident. Cathy could only think that he was speaking to someone from the hospital about Jody.

'Yes, I understand... OK, I'll ring later this evening.' He replaced the receiver and turned with a smile. 'Jody is out of the coma.'

'That's really good news,' Cathy said sincerely and then reached over to Poppy. 'Do you hear that? Your mummy is getting better. She'll be coming home to you soon.'

Poppy gurgled as if she could understand every word.

Cathy was pleased. She had hated to think of Poppy being without her mother, but there was a part of her that instantly wondered what would happen now. 'So, do you think they will be discharging Ms Sterling from hospital soon?' she asked curiously.

'It's early days yet.' Pearce's manner changed from euphoric to guarded. 'But the doctors are hopeful—all her vital signs are looking good.'

'You must be so relieved...'

'I am. I just wish I could go and see her.' He raked a hand through his hair in a frustrated way. 'If it wasn't for this damn air strike I'd be flying to her now.'

Some strange emotion stirred inside Cathy. She didn't understand the feeling. She was genuinely glad that Jody was on her way to recovery yet, when Pearce spoke like that, there was a tug of something almost like envy inside her. She sucked in her breath at such a ridiculous notion and immediately swept such foolish nonsense out of her mind.

Pearce glanced at his watch then got to his feet. 'I have a few important telephone calls to make before we go into Antibes to collect your luggage.'

Immediately Cathy started to feel nervous—she had hoped that Pearce would change his mind about the trip into town. She didn't want him to accompany her. She needed time to phone Mike, and pack up some things at the hotel. Having Pearce with her would make things very difficult.

'Do you think we should bring Poppy?' she asked in an attempt to change his mind. 'The heat of the car might not be so good for her. And there doesn't seem much point in us all going. I can be there and back in no time—'

'My car is air-conditioned and I have business in Antibes anyway,' he interrupted her, his tone dismissive.

Cathy realised that there was no arguing with Pearce when his mind was made up, so she just shrugged. Now all she had to do was come up with an idea on how she could lose him in Antibes, she thought despondently. If he saw her going into her hotel he would be immediately suspicious.

She watched as he picked Poppy up from her high chair, a look of tender indulgence on his face. 'Come on, sweetheart,' he said gently. 'You can come and keep me company while I make my phone calls.' He kissed the upturned little face affectionately and Poppy awarded him a cute, dimpled smile.

Cathy watched them go, trying to ignore the way her heart suddenly seemed to constrict. She like the way Pearce doted on Poppy... It was crazy but it seemed to draw her irresistibly towards him.

She got up from the table with a sigh. There were a lot of complex emotions clouding her work here. She didn't even begin to understand some of the feelings Pearce seemed to create in her. All she knew was that she had to put a lid on the cauldron, otherwise she would never be able to write her story.

Swiftly Cathy tidied away the breakfast dishes. Then she made up a bottle for Poppy in case she was hungry whilst they were out.

When she stepped out of the kitchen the first thing she heard was Poppy's laughter. The hearty chuckles were infectious and, filled with curiosity, she followed them down towards Pearce's study.

His door was open and she peeped in cautiously. He was sitting in his office chair but he had pushed it away from the desk so that he was beside the open French doors. Poppy was on his knee and he was bouncing her gently up and down. The child was loving every moment of the game, and every time he stopped she gave a little murmur of protest until he started again and then she laughed and laughed.

Cathy noticed the way his large hands held the small child so carefully, so protectively, the way he smiled at the baby, the way he seemed to be enjoying himself.

'You seem to be having fun,' she said lightly as Pearce glanced over and saw her.

'We are.' He smiled warmly at her. 'Come in.'

She wished that he wouldn't smile at her like that. It made her just want to melt. 'Have you made your phone calls?' She crossed to stand by his desk, trying to sound nonchalant—trying to sound as if he didn't have such a heady effect on her senses.

'Yes, I have.' He stood up and she noticed a book that had been tucked down beside him in the chair. Impulsively she reached to pick it up. *Modern-Day*

Child. She read the title aloud and then looked over at him with a raised eyebrow. 'Doing a little research?'

'You probably know all there is to know about babies...' He grinned at her...but when you are a complete novice like me you need all the help you can get.'

Was this the man that only yesterday she had thought of as cold and aloof? She flicked through the pages and noticed that there was a bookmark on the chapter on teething. 'You are a very surprising man, Pearce Tyrone,' she murmured thoughtfully, almost to herself.

'Why's that?' He sounded amused.

'Well...' She shrugged. 'I didn't think a busy man like you would take the time to read up on babies.'

He smiled at that. 'That's a rather sexist remark, if I might say so, Catherine.'

'Perhaps it is.' The more she got to know Pearce Tyrone the more she got to like him...and the more she started to think that Jody Sterling was really a very lucky woman. She met his eyes and a frisson of awareness seemed to sneak surreptitiously through her body.

'Should we go into Antibes now?' She moved abruptly away from him, danger signals starting to build up inside. She was here to work, she told herself fiercely... Under no circumstances could she allow herself to start getting emotionally involved—on any level.

Half an hour later Cathy sat in the passenger seat of Pearce's Mercedes as they drove towards Antibes. It was a beautiful day and the sky was a cloudless azure blue— a fabulous backdrop for spectacular countryside.

They took a different route from the one Cathy had originally taken to Pearce's villa, heading inland for a little while. Cathy drank in the scenery, wishing that she could tell Pearce to slow down, to stop even. She stared out at fields of lavender in straight, regimented rows of purple against the red earth, at villages perched precari-

ously on mountain-tops, seemingly unchanged by modern-day life.

Everywhere was so dreamily perfect that it was hell
to know that she was not going to have time to explore—
that she probably wouldn't see anything of the South of
France now. She was halfway through her week's vacation as it was.

'It's so beautiful,' she murmured wistfully, almost to
herself.

Pearce glanced across at her and slowed the car.
'Probably one of the most beautiful places on earth.' he
agreed. 'Have you had much of a chance to look around
while you've been working out here?'

She shook her head. She didn't want to get into a
conversation about her 'work' out here.

'Pity, it warrants some time.'

'That's something you don't seem to get a lot of when
you're a nanny.' She couldn't resist the dig.

He gave her a sideways glance. 'How many days off
did your previous employer give you?'

'More than you do.' She smiled.

'So, if they were so wonderful, why did you quit?'

'Well…' Cathy cursed herself for heading into this
minefield and racked her brains for a reply. Hadn't she
already told him why she had left? She didn't like lying,
she was no good at it. 'The child I was looking after is
old enough to go to boarding school now, so my services
are no longer required,' she murmured finally.

'I see. English family, are they? Maybe I know them.'

'Oh, no!' Cathy shook her head firmly. 'I don't think
you would know them.' Heavens, she should never have
started this, she thought frantically. She should have told
him that she had flown directly in from London and had
lost her luggage.

'Why not? I have a few friends who live in Antibes.'

'Well, these people are French,' Cathy said desperately.

'I have lots of French friends. What's their name?'

Cathy's mind went an awful blank. She couldn't for the life of her think of a French name off the top of her head.

'I said, "What's their name?"' Pearce gave her an odd look as she made no answer.

'Dubonnet.' It was the only French name she could think of.

'Dubonnet?' His lips curved in a sardonic kind of smile.

'Mmm, like the drink.' She tried to sound nonchalant.

'And how long have you worked for the Dubonnet family?' he asked coolly.

Cathy couldn't believe that she had chosen such a name. How could she have been so daft as to choose the name of a drink...it certainly didn't sound bona fide. 'Oh, about a year,' she answered airily.

'So you must be good at speaking French?' He spoke the words in French, his accent fluent.

'Not bad. I can get by.' She answered him in French, her accent passable. Thank heavens she had studied hard in French class, she thought with a sigh.

He slowed the car as they rounded a very steep bend and Cathy took the opportunity to change the conversation. 'Where did Jody Sterling have her accident?' She knew very well that Jody's car crash had been in Paris and that was where she was in hospital, but it was the only way she could think to introduce the subject.

'Don't you read the papers?' He slanted another sideways glance at her, his eyes suddenly hard.

'Not very often.' She shrugged.

'I can't say I blame you,' He raked an impatient hand through his dark hair. 'You can't believe a word they print most of the time anyway. I'm sure half these reporters would sell their grandmother for a story—it wouldn't have to be a true story either.'

'Well, I wouldn't agree with that.' Cathy protested. 'I think a lot of journalists go to a great deal of trouble in search of the truth. If it wasn't for them the world would be ignorant to a lot of injustices that go on.'

'But it doesn't stop there, does it, Ms Fielding? They poke and pry into people's privacy, not caring what havoc they create. And, at the end of the day, it's not for the greater good of the people that they do these things, it's for the love of money.'

The bitter note to his voice didn't escape Cathy's notice. Obviously Pearce Tyrone was not a lover of the press but, then, she supposed she already knew that.

A curl of guilt stirred again inside her. She was prying into Pearce's privacy and it was for no other reason than to feed her paper with gossip. This wasn't her usual kind of assignment at all and if she was honest it wasn't something she really wanted to do...but, then, work was work and having a conscience didn't help much when the bills dropped through the door.

'And to answer your question. Jody Sterling had her accident in Paris.'

'Oh.' Cathy should have followed up quickly by asking more probing questions, but her enthusiasm was dulled by an attack of moral deliberation on the ethics of the situation.

'So what will happen when the time comes for Ms Sterling to be discharged from hospital?' she asked finally. 'I mean, I don't suppose you will need a nanny then, not if Poppy is going back to her mother? Or will Ms Sterling come down here to recuperate?'

'Ah...I wondered when you would get around to asking that,' Pearce drawled.

'You did?' She turned wide, innocent eyes on him. 'Why is that?'

'Because it's obvious you would worry about your job, of course.'

'And do I need to worry? Will Poppy be going back?'

He hesitated for a moment, then smiled silkily. 'Let's just take it a day at a time…shall we?'

The man could be infuriatingly vague. 'Well, I need to know,' she persisted doggedly. 'I mean, it's only right that you give me some notice so that I can arrange another job with the agency—'

'Don't worry, Ms Fielding. I'll make sure you are well taken care of when the time comes for you to leave.'

For some reason that statement didn't sound very reassuring, but that was probably because she was having feelings of misgivings. When it was time for her to leave here Pearce would probably know that she was a reporter, and all hell would be breaking loose.

She remembered his words in the office yesterday about suing any newspaper that printed anything incorrect about him and she shuddered. She was going to have to be very careful.

'You were calling me Catherine earlier,' she reminded him softly, and gave him one of her brightest smiles. 'It sounds so formal when you keep calling me Ms Fielding.'

On most occasions when Cathy turned on her gentle approach and her soft smile men melted. Pearce Tyrone, however, seemed to be the exception. His blue eyes hardened, his lips set in a firm look of disapproval. 'They went in for informality a lot at your nanny training school, I take it?' he grated.

She sat back, totally flattened by his manner. 'Well, we were told that the days of keeping the servants below stairs were over,' she told him sarcastically.

'Did they also tell you to walk around the nursery with very few clothes on?' Pearce's lips twisted in a half teasing, half mocking way.

Her skin flared with heat. 'I told you, I forgot my night things.'

'So you did.' He sounded unconvinced. Cathy would have said more on the subject but Poppy started to cry.

Twisting around in her seat she looked at the little girl who was strapped carefully into her child seat.

'What's the matter with her?' Pearce slowed the car.

'It's all right. Her dummy has fallen out.' Cathy retrieved it and handed it back to Poppy and silence fell once more in the car.

They didn't speak again until they reached the perimeters of Antibes, and then Pearce asked her for the address.

'Address?' She was momentarily at a loss as she forgot what she was doing.

'The Dubonnet family,' he reminded her drily. 'Where do they live?'

'Oh, yes…along here.' She waved to the road ahead. 'Don't…don't worry, I'll direct you.'

'I'm not worried,' he assured her, a droll smile playing along his firm lips.

No, but I am, Cathy thought nervously. Her plan was to ask him to drop her off just around the corner from the hotel, then she would tell him that it would take her half an hour to pack her bags and that she would meet him back on the corner again. That way she should have time to get her things together and ring Mike.

'What's the name of the road?' Pearce asked patiently.

She had been afraid that he was going to ask that. She didn't have a clue about the names of streets…only the one her hotel was on and she didn't want him stopping there because it was much too risky. If he saw her going in or coming out of that hotel his suspicions would be instantly aroused.

'Do you know, I can't remember?' She frowned, pretending to think. 'But it's along here.' She waved him forward. 'And the first turning left.'

'I can't turn left. It's a no-entry.'

'Oh, dear. Well, I'll tell you what...you can drop me here. I'll be about half an hour putting my things together and you can pick me up here when you've seen to your business in town.' She hoped that she wasn't babbling nervously because she certainly felt as if she was. The deception was making her feel quite ill.

'Nonsense, I can't allow you to walk with heavy bags.' Pearce took the second turning. 'I'll drive in from the other end. What number house is it?'

Cathy's heart hammered furiously. She needed him to turn chivalrous now like she needed a hole in the head. 'I'll...I'll show you.' She waved her hand airily forward again, ignoring the fact that they had just sailed past the front of her hotel. Desperately she tried to remember the houses on the next street, wondering which would be safest to choose as her bogus address.

'Here will do,' she said as they rounded the corner.

'Here?' He looked at the large house which was half-hidden by high walls and a massive wrought-iron gate.

'Yes, thank you.' She reached for the door handle. 'Will you be able to pick me up here in half an hour?'

'It's OK, I'll wait.' To her horror, he reached to switch off the engine.

'Oh no...don't do that. I hate to think of you just sitting here, wasting your time,' she said hurriedly. 'Really, you go and see to your business.'

'It's no trouble.' He turned off the engine and sat back in his seat. 'I'm sure it won't take you half an hour to get your things together, anyway.'

'Oh, it will...I've got lots of clothes and—'

'Get going, Catherine.' He cut across her firmly. 'Otherwise we will be sitting here all day.'

There was no arguing with that tone of voice. Her

heart thudding wildly, she climbed out of the car and stood in front of the gates. What in the hell was she going to do now? she wondered frantically. March up to the house and confront some total stranger? And what could she say...I've come to read the meter? This was a mess, an absolute mess.

At least Pearce wouldn't be able to see her once she was at the front door, that was if she was even able to get to the front door. How did the gates open? she wondered, studying the heavy latch with complete mystification.

The electric windows wound down on the car behind her. 'It might help if you pressed the bell,' Pearce suggested drily.

'I was just about to.' She flashed him a glaring, impatient look. Did he have to sit there, watching her every move? And he looked so damn smug, into the bargain, that her fingers itched to wipe that superior smile off his face.

Taking a deep breath, she controlled the irate anger boiling up inside her and glanced around for the bell. It was no wonder she hadn't been able to see it—it was half-hidden by a creeper on the gate post. Trust Pearce Tyrone to notice it. Nothing seemed to escape that man's attention.

She pushed it and after a couple of minutes the gates ground open electronically.

Well, here goes, Cathy thought nervously as she stepped through. Just what she was going to say to the people in here she had no idea...and what would Pearce say when she returned empty-handed. Perhaps she could tell him that the Dubonnet family had had a burglary and that all her stuff had been stolen. That was the thing about lying, she thought grimly. One small lie always led to another and before you knew where you were you had dug yourself one almighty big grave.

The gates closed again behind her with an ominous clanking sound, making her look around in alarm.

'Look, you are probably right,' Pearce said suddenly. 'There's no point in my sitting here. I'll pick you up in half an hour.'

'Oh, great.' Cathy tried to keep the ironic edge out of her voice. It was just her luck that he should wait until she was locked inside before saying that. She sighed and waved a hand as he drove off. At least she had some chance of getting around to the hotel now, but first she had to get out of here which would take up valuable time. At this rate she would have no time for her phone call.

'Can I help you?' an old man called to her in French from the doorway of the house.

'Sorry, I've got the wrong house.' Cathy stood patiently while the man came slowly out towards her. At this rate, she could kiss goodbye to her luggage as well as her phone call, she thought with dismay.

Cathy was out of breath when she finally got to her hotel. She had fifteen minutes to do everything. She ran around her bedroom, flinging things into her case in an untidy heap. Consequentially it was hard to shut the lid on it. She forced it down by sitting on it and at the same time dialled Mike's number at the paper.

'Cathy, where the hell have you been?' he rasped angrily when she finally got through. 'I've been trying to get hold of you for hours.'

'Inside Pearce Tyrone's house.' She got to the point quickly. 'Somehow he's mistaken me for Poppy's nanny.'

'You're joking!' Her editor sounded stunned. 'Hell, that's wonderful... Good work—'

'It's not so wonderful, believe me,' Cathy interrupted. 'To be honest, I don't know how long I can keep up the pretence.'

'Have you seen the child?'

'Of course I've seen Poppy. I'm looking after her,' Cathy said with exasperation.

'And photographs...have you got photographs?' Mike totally ignored her sarcasm.

'Well, a few—'

'We need pictures. Especially some of Tyrone with the child. They are a priority.'

'I can't take any photographs openly of Pearce and Poppy. It's difficult, Mike—'

'Of course it's not difficult,' Mike spluttered angrily. 'Listen, you need a good photographer. I'll organise someone—'

'No, Mike, don't send anyone,' Cathy interjected in panic. 'I'd never get anyone else into the house. I'm on borrowed time there myself.'

'For heaven's sake, Cathy, you are a professional. You could think of some way around the problems. Tell Tyrone you want your boyfriend to visit or something,' Mike grated heatedly. 'It's a pity about this air strike, but I might have someone in Italy we could use. He could take the train down.'

'No, Mike...it's too risky. Look, I've got to go—'

'I'll ring you at Tyrone's house,' Mike told her firmly. 'Do you know the number?'

'No, I do not... Don't ring me, Mike. Pearce will be suspicious.'

'Don't be silly. You are an attractive woman. You are bound to have a boyfriend who wants to phone you. What name are you using?'

'My own but, Mike, please don't ring. I'm in a dangerous situation.'

'And I know how you love danger,' her boss laughed. 'Weren't you the girl who begged to be sent out to a war zone last year?'

'Yes, but that was different—' Or was it? she found

herself wondering with a kind of hysterical humour. She glanced at her watch and panicked. 'Got to go. Mike—'

'Have you heard that Jody Sterling is making a complete recovery?' Mike asked now. 'And it is common knowledge that Poppy is with Pearce Tyrone.'

'Damn!' That was bad news. Now Pearce would be inundated by reporters, all wanting the inside story, and it would be a race to get the details and print first.

'There's a rumour that Jody will be going down to the South of France as soon as she is fit to travel. Have you found out what Pearce's feelings are for her? Do you think he might ask her to marry him?'

'Marry him?' Cathy repeated his question dazedly. 'I don't think so—'

'For heaven's sake, Cathy, pull your finger out. It's imperative that you find out. The man has a child with Jody. It's odds on there are wedding bells in the air—a happy ending. Find out. I want that story first.'

Cathy sighed and glanced at her watch. 'I don't like this, Mike... I feel dishonest.'

Her editor totally ignored that. 'Have you found out anything interesting at all?'

She could at that juncture have mentioned the fact that Pearce had been married before, but she didn't. 'I'm working on it' was all she said, her tone flat.

'I don't care what you have to do. Just get a good story.' Mike ground the words out, a veiled threat of her job hanging in the air between them.

Cathy slammed the phone down. Mike was starting to really annoy her. She was beginning to feel that it wouldn't be long before she picked up his hidden threats and threw them back at him, telling him to keep his job. The only thing that stopped her was that she loved reporting so much. It had seen her through some very lonely, very tough times.

She pictured Mike for a moment. He was a very hard

man. His wife had been heard to complain that Mike would even sell her for a good story. Cathy had laughed at that...but lately she was starting to wonder if it wasn't closer to the truth than she had thought.

Glaring at her watch, she picked up her suitcase and fled towards the lift. She was already late for Pearce's deadline.

When she got back outside and rounded the corner towards the place where Pearce had left her, she was dismayed to see that his car was already there. It was a relief when she noticed that at least he was still sitting in it. If Pearce had gone into that house it would all be over now.

'Hi.' She summoned a bright smile as he got out of the car, knowing that she was going to have to explain why she was walking around the streets with her luggage.

'Where have you been?'

He didn't waste time with pleasantries, Cathy noticed derisively.

'You weren't here when I came out so I just went around the corner to buy...something,' she said breathlessly.

'Buy what?' He took her case from her and put it in the boot of the car.

She would dearly have liked to tell him to mind his own business, but one look at his face made her think twice. He looked quite formidable, his lips in a firm line and his eyes very serious.

'Personal items, if you must know,' she grated with annoyance. Let him make what he wanted of that.

For a moment she thought that he was going to ask her what personal items. She held her breath, wondering what she should say, but thankfully the question didn't come. He reached past her and opened the passenger door. 'Let's go, then.'

Cathy was silent for most of the journey home, her mind on her conversation with Mike. She hoped that he wasn't going to send a photographer—it would be too difficult for words.

She tried not to dwell on the fact that she hadn't passed on the information about Pearce being a widower. She didn't know why she hadn't told Mike. It had been more a feeling inside her than a deliberate omission.

Pearce muttered something under his breath, bringing her attention sharply back to him.

'Looks like we've got company,' he said in answer to her look of enquiry as he slowed the car.

She glanced ahead. She shouldn't have been shocked by the crowd of reporters awaiting their approach to the gates of Pearce's villa, but she was. Cameras eagerly turned in their direction as they pulled up and she cursed inwardly. Mike had been right when he had told her that the story had already broken.

Pearce sounded his hooter impatiently as he edged his car towards the crowd. It made little impact towards clearing a path for them. Half the reporters stood their ground in front of the bonnet of the car while others clamoured at the windows, all of them asking the same questions.

'Is there any truth in the rumour that you and Jody are planning to get married now? Are you Poppy's father?'

Pearce didn't even glance sideways at them. He just continued to allow the car to roll forward very gently, his hand pressed firmly on the hooter until the reporters in front had no alternative but to move away.

Cathy shrank down in her seat, nervous in case any of them recognised her. She tried to avert her face as cameras flashed in her direction.

As she turned her head sharply she thought she recognised a face amongst the crowd. It was just a fleeting glimpse of a good-looking, fair-haired man, but her whole body went into turmoil.

She hadn't seen David Collins since the day he had walked out of her life two years ago. It couldn't have been David, Cathy told herself sternly. The last she had heard, he was working as a freelance photographic journalist in Germany. She didn't dare scan the crowd again, just sank even lower in her seat.

Pearce pressed his automatic control to let the gates open. 'Damn vultures,' he muttered angrily once they were safely through.

Cathy shivered at the note of fury in his voice, struck once more by his low regard for members of the press. Heaven help her when he discovered that she was one of the set he despised so much. She could only hope that she would be miles away when he finally discovered the truth. 'I'm sure they are just trying to do their jobs,' she said in a conciliatory tone.

'You think so?' He shot her an impatient look and then frowned. 'What's the matter? You look very pale.'

'Nothing is the matter.' She sat up straighter as the car moved well away from the gates. She was starting to feel foolish now. It hadn't been David Collins, she told herself again. Her ex-fiancé was miles away and he was history.

'I detest the damned press,' Pearce muttered irately as he glanced to check that Poppy was all right in the back seat. The little girl was fast asleep, her head resting against the child seat, her lashes dark against the creamy softness of her skin.

'Frankly, I think they enjoy stirring up trouble.' He pulled the car to a standstill in front of the house. 'I mean, who the hell is interested in whether I marry Jody Sterling or not, anyway?'

I am, Cathy thought as she shrugged lightly and pretended to look vague.

'Surely people have more important things to worry about?' Pearce continued sardonically. 'And I suppose that because I didn't stop and make some reply to their questions they will just make up some answers.' He slanted a look at her. 'They will probably say that you and I are having an affair.'

'I hardly think so,' Cathy replied stiffly, something about the very suggestion making her feel hot and awkward.

'Don't you? I tell you these people have no scruples.'

Cathy's temper rose sharply at that remark. 'They are not all like that,' she said crossly, but even as she spoke she was aware that her very presence here thrust her firmly into the category of journalists he so despised. 'And, anyway, if you wanted to live in anonymity you should have become a plumber or something.' She glared at him, her eyes glimmering like deep chips of emerald.

'Is that a fact?' A gleam of amusement played over his handsome features.

'It's a fact that it's basic human nature to be curious. People are interested in people, especially famous people.' She didn't notice his amusement—she was too fired up. 'I mean, haven't you ever wondered about anyone? Haven't you ever wanted to take a look behind the scenes—find out what makes an interesting character, what motivates them, what makes them tick?'

'And you think you would find that out just by reading an article in the paper?' he asked drolly, then shook his head. 'That's rather naïve of you. I'm afraid I'm rather more of a sceptic. I reckon that half the stuff that is printed in the papers is fabricated, anyway. If they haven't got enough meaty information they spice their stories by twisting and distorting the truth.'

She opened her mouth to tell him that she had never twisted the truth in her life, that she prided herself in telling a fair and accurate story. The words hovered precariously on the edge of her tongue when suddenly she realised what she was doing. She had very nearly thrown away her chances of getting any story at all in the heat of an emotional moment. She closed her mouth and moistened her lips nervously, hardly able to believe what she had nearly done.

'You were about to say something?' Pearce lifted one eyebrow and fixed her with a hard look of enquiry, taking in the sudden vulnerable light in her eyes.

'No, nothing.' She shook her head. 'Just…just that everyone has to make a living.'

'So you think it was cruel of me not to throw them some kind of comment?'

'Well…' She shrugged, at a loss. 'You could have told them something.'

'You could be right. I like to think of myself as a reasonable man.'

Before she could say anything he put the car in reverse. For a startled moment she thought that he was going to drive back down to the reporters, but he merely turned the vehicle so that they were facing the gates and switched off the ignition again.

'Let's give them something to write about, then, shall we?'

She looked over at him, a frown marring the smoothness of her forehead. 'What do you mean?'

He reached out and put a hand under her chin, tipping her face up further towards his. 'I mean that if I kiss you they might all go home happy.' His voice had lowered to a husky tone.

She stared up at him, and a frisson of awareness stole through her body as her eyes met his.

'I…I don't think that is…such a good idea,' she murmured nervously, her eyes moving to his lips. Her heart felt as if it was beating out of control and her breathing felt suddenly restricted.

'Why not?' There was a warm, teasing quality about his voice. 'Are you afraid...or maybe it's not politically correct to be seen kissing your employer?'

From somewhere she drew on the sanity to ask, 'And how would you explain the kiss to Jody Sterling?'

'I don't think I need to explain myself to anyone.' He shrugged nonchalantly. 'But, since you ask, I'd say it was an exercise in pleasing the press.'

Her eyes narrowed, but before she could make any reply he moved even closer and his lips covered hers.

She meant to pull away sharply—she could have very easily. She could have slapped him across the face. But instead she kissed him back.

His lips were softly caressing, sending whispering flares of desire shooting through her. They made her want to melt into him.

'Mmm, nice exercise,' he murmured as he pulled back from her.

Cathy felt as if her body didn't belong to her. The kiss could only have lasted a few seconds but he had stirred something up inside her, something that filled her with so many traitorous longings that she felt confused, dizzy with them.

'I don't believe that we did that,' she said huskily.

'Don't you?' His eyes moved over the soft curve of her lips and she felt herself tremble as if he had kissed her again. 'We could always have an action replay, just in case someone didn't have their zoom lens working.'

Suddenly everything was sharply pulled into focus again. 'You do realise that kiss was totally crazy?'

'Oh, yes.' His voice was all at once very serious, all traces of his previous joviality gone. 'Totally crazy.'

Her eyes skirted away from him and down towards the gates. 'Do you think anyone will have got a decent

photo at this distance?' she asked nervously. The thought
that her photograph might be plastered all over the newspapers tomorrow made her feel very alarmed. If her editor saw it he would wonder just what was going on. Then
there was the fear of someone recognising her.

'I sincerely hope they did.' He opened the door and
got out. 'With a bit of luck, someone will make a good
story out of it.'

'And so take the emphasis off the issue of your marriage to Jody Sterling?' The question was ugly but she
felt compelled to ask it. 'Was that kiss a message for
Jody as well as for the press? Are you trying to tell her
that you are not going to marry her?'

He glanced across the roof of the car at her as she
climbed out into the warm heat of the sun. He observed
the glimmer of fury in her eyes, the soft tremor of her
lower lip. 'Catherine, you are taking the whole thing too
seriously,' he said laconically.

'And Jody won't?'

'You want an honest answer to that?' His lips twisted
in an amused, sardonic way.

'Are you capable of giving one?' She watched as he
tenderly lifted the sleeping Poppy from the back of the
car and suddenly she felt like crying.

He hesitated and she could see that there was an indecision in his eyes for just a moment. Then he said
clearly, 'There is no question of my marrying Jody
Sterling. She knows that, I know that, and the press will
know it now.'

She had her answer, but it opened up so many other
questions.

CHAPTER SIX

CATHY had tried really hard with dinner. Now she felt like throwing all the saucepans out of the window as one by one everything started to go wrong. The sauce boiled over, the vegetables were overcooked.

'How's dinner going?' Pearce came into the kitchen just as she was putting a burnt pan in the sink. 'Wonderful.' She turned, her manner overbright—her body positioned in front of the offending kitchen equipment.

'Have I got time for a shower?' His eyes moved to the stove and the simmering pots.

'Oh, yes, take your time.'

She felt like collapsing in a heap as he left the room.

It had been a hard day. Poppy had been demanding and then there was the tension that was lingering in the air. She needed to serve Pearce a burnt dinner now like she needed Mike to suddenly appear at the door.

Since that kiss there had been a definite coolness between them. She had worked for an hour, typing out notes in his study this afternoon, and he had barely spoken except in a clipped, formal tone.

She had found herself watching him at one point, her eyes moving over his handsome features as she tried to fathom him out. She had come to the conclusion that he was worried that she had read too much into their kiss—that she had got the wrong idea—when, in fact, it had just been a bit of frivolous fun.

She placed a hand to her lips almost as if she could feel them tingling the way they had when he had caressed them. She was under no illusions that Pearce had meant anything serious by the gesture, but she wished that she could stop thinking about it.

She turned away from the sink and crossed purposefully towards the telephone.

She wasn't even going to bother trying to cook any more. An idea had occurred to her earlier, an idea that she had dismissed as being too risky. But now that Pearce had gone for a shower and the press had disappeared from the front gates...she flicked a glance at the monitors to make sure that was still the case. Yes, the driveway was completely clear. Now that it was quiet she was going to take a chance.

With determination she picked up the telephone directory and found the number for a small bistro, Le Gardin, that was just a few miles down the road. She knew they would deliver—she had already phoned earlier to enquire.

She would leave the gates open for them and ask them to deliver the food around the back of the house to the kitchen door. Pearce need never be any the wiser.

Cathy's sense of bravado deserted her almost completely when Pearce returned to the kitchen before their food had arrived.

He looked very attractive in a casual way. He was wearing a pair of jeans and a pale blue silk shirt, his hair still slightly damp from the shower.

'Can I give you a hand with anything?' he asked, his gaze going towards the oven.

'No...no, thank you.' She prayed that he wouldn't glance towards the end of the kitchen at the TV monitors because if he did he would notice that the front gates were wide open. 'You go on into your study and I'll bring your dinner through on a tray, if you like,' she offered in a desperate attempt to get him out of the room.

'I've done enough work for one day.' He pulled out

one of the kitchen chairs and sat down. 'If it's all right with you, I thought we could eat together.'

Her nervous system jumped in a very precarious way. Part of her was pleased by the suggestion but, then, if he stayed in here he was going to find out that she had ordered dinner. Very soon now there would be the sound of a car engine and the delivery man would knock on the back door.

'That is a nice idea.' She bit down on her lip, her mind trying to come up with some way of getting him out of the kitchen. 'Why don't we eat in the dining-room?' she suggested brightly. 'It will be much more relaxing for you.'

'Well, I'm all for being relaxed.' There was a kind of lazy amusement in his tone that was somehow provocative.

She was acutely conscious of him, almost to the point where she could feel his eyes moving over her.

After she had settled Poppy down in her cot for the night she had changed into a short black skirt and a white blouse in a soft silky jersey material. They had been the only items of clothing that hadn't been creased from the way she had jammed them into her case.

Now she found herself wondering if her skirt was too short. The sudden idea that Pearce would think that she was deliberately flaunting herself, just as he had last night, make her cheeks burn with uncomfortable heat.

'So, would you like to go on through to the other room?' she asked nervously.

'OK.' To her relief, he stood up, but he didn't leave immediately. Instead, he started to open the cutlery drawer and then he took some glasses from one of the cupboards.

'May as well lay the table,' he said in answer to her tense enquiry.

Cathy watched him, her ears straining for the sound of a car engine, while her nerves stretched.

It seemed that he had only just walked out of the kitchen when she heard the sound of the car. Quickly she stepped out into the warmth of the night air.

The delivery man must have thought she was crazy because she grabbed the boxes from him and shoved the money into his hand. Then she raced back into the house.

'You're a good cook, Catherine,' Pearce commented as she put the second course down in front of him.

'Thank you.' She hoped that he would put her high colour down to the fact that she had been slaving over a hot stove.

They were sitting at the polished rosewood table in the elegant dining-room. Pearce had lit the candles on the table and the sideboard and the flickering light gave an intimacy to the meal that was unsettling.

The evening had a special feel about it, as if they were two lovers enjoying a meal together. Once the thought had crossed Cathy's mind she could barely bring herself to look at Pearce. It was a ludicrous notion. He had wanted to dine in the kitchen—this had been her idea.

She wondered if he thought her presumptuous for suggesting it. If he was now wondering if she had gone completely overboard because of that kiss.

She was very concerned about what he thought of her. It was absurd under the circumstances—he was going to think a lot worse when he discovered the truth. 'You didn't need to go to the trouble of lighting the candles,' she told him in an attempt at making the situation more normal.

'Well, you went to the trouble of cooking a lovely meal.' He looked up at her with a smile. 'And you did suggest that we eat in here. So we may as well do so in style.'

'Yes.' She was silent for just a moment, her mind spinning. 'But when I suggested we ate in here I wasn't...' She trailed off, unsure of what she was saying. 'I mean...I don't want you to think...' She stopped. She was making matters worse.

Their eyes met across the table. He looked amused, but in a tender, indulgent way that made her heart dip wildly. She swallowed hard. 'I suppose what I'm trying to say is that I feel uncomfortable because of...this afternoon—'

'Because we kissed?' He went straight to the point— it was most disconcerting.

She nodded. 'I know there was nothing meant by it. I know it was just a flirtatious bit of fun.' She shrugged almost helplessly. 'I just want you to know that I know...' She trailed off and shrugged again. 'Am I making any sense?'

'Not really.' He laughed. It was a warm sound. It did something to Cathy's pulse rate.

He leaned across and poured a glass of rich red wine into her glass. The candlelight gleamed on the mellow fruity red and the exquisite cut glass.

'How do you know that I didn't mean anything by it anyway?' he asked suddenly.

Her hand stilled on the silver cutlery. 'Don't tease, Pearce. It isn't funny and it isn't gallant.'

'I don't know if I want to be gallant. You are a very attractive woman, Catherine. You have a way of disturbing a man's equanimity.'

The seriousness of his tone caused a shiver to race down her back. She realised in that instant that Pearce was probably a master at the art of seduction. He had all the attributes—a fabulous body, a handsome face, a smooth tongue when it suited him.

She shook her head, trying to dispel the sensual aura that he was creating with his words. 'And didn't you say something about not fraternising with the staff?' She tried to laugh away the moment but her laughter fell flat.

'Yes, I did, and perhaps that statement was levelled more at myself—to make me keep my distance from you.'

Now she felt totally out of her depth.

He looked so very enticing. There was something about the dark thickness of his hair, the way a lock of it fell over his forehead, that made her want to reach out and brush it back with her fingertips.

'Do you have a serious man in your life, Catherine?' he asked suddenly.

He sounded as if he was genuinely interested in her and it took her aback for a second. 'No. No one serious. Not since...not for a long time,' she finished the sentence awkwardly. She had been about to say, not since David. But she didn't want to get into conversation about her ex-fiancé. She remembered how she had thought she had seen him outside the gates of the house earlier. She had been mistaken, of course, but the notion had been disturbing.

'You were about to say, not since your engagement ended?'

Pearce was nothing if not perceptive, she thought warily as she met his eyes. She inclined her head.

'How long ago is it since you split up?'

'About two years.' She reached for her wine glass. Any moment now he was going to ask where she and David had met. As they had worked together for the newspaper, she didn't want to start treading over dangerous ground and inventing stories so she said abruptly, 'Do you mind if we change the subject? I don't really like talking about David.'

'Why? Aren't you over him?'

'Oh, yes…long ago.' She fixed him with a direct, unwavering look. 'I just don't like the subject.'

'He must have hurt you a lot.' His eyes moved over her face, lingering for just a moment too long on the soft fullness of her lips. 'The man must have been crazy to let you go.'

The words and the way he spoke them did very strange things to her emotions.

Then he smiled and she wondered dazedly if he was well aware of the effect he was having on her. 'So, what would you like to talk about?' he asked.

For a moment she had difficulty getting her brain into a businesslike frame. It was fogged with the fervid emotions he had stirred up so easily. 'I don't know…' She shrugged helplessly. 'Poppy? Tell me about her mother. What is she like?'

He frowned and she wondered if she had approached the subject clumsily. She certainly felt as if she had.

'Jody is beautiful, talented.' He reached for his wine. 'But surely you have seen her in films?'

'Yes.' She nodded. 'I was just curious as to what the real Jody Sterling was like.'

'She's a lovely person. There is not much more to add.' His tone was abrupt.

Perhaps she should have taken the hint and dropped the subject, but she didn't want to. 'So, why aren't you going to marry her?'

'Is this the natural human curiosity that you were talking about this afternoon?' he asked aridly. 'Or are you taking a more personal interest?'

'I'm just curious.' She kept her tone carefully light.

The sooner she got a clear picture of the situation between him and the actress the sooner she could start penning her article, and then this charade would be over and she could leave. The thought created an unwelcome curl of deep regret that she found profoundly disturbing.

'If you buy the newspapers tomorrow I'm sure they will have a few ideas on that for you.'

'I didn't really want the newspapers' ideas,' she said candidly. 'And, anyway, if they managed to get a photograph of...us this afternoon I know what they will be saying.'

'That I am a cad and a womaniser.' He leaned back in his chair, a small smile playing around his lips.

'And are you?'

'Now, there is a loaded question. If I say no you won't believe me...will you? Not after the way I've just told you that I find you attractive...the way I kissed you this afternoon.' He leaned forward, his elbows resting on the table as he looked into her eyes. 'Although I have to say that I noticed that the passion that flared when our lips met wasn't entirely one-sided.'

She tried not to look flustered by the directness of that remark, but she felt decidedly ruffled. She had enjoyed the feel of his lips against hers. Even thinking about it now sent latent desire swirling inside her. 'Perhaps that is wishful thinking on your behalf,' she answered, trying to inject a prim, disapproving note into the proceedings.

He laughed at that. 'If you say so.' He didn't sound in the slightest bit convinced. 'So, if I answer, yes, I am a womaniser, you are going to be worried that I will kiss you again...aren't you?'

'I think that you are deliberately taunting me.' She set down her glass. 'You are deliberately trying to embarrass me...wind me up, aren't you?'

'Am I?' His voice was cool, his features impassive. 'And am I succeeding?'

'No.' Her smile was forced, her voice emphatic.

'Well, that's all right, then.' He sounded pleased with himself. He knew damn well he was disturbing her senses, Cathy thought furiously.

Her eyes moved over him reflectively. She still hadn't

got any deep answers from him about his relationship with Jody and why he wasn't going to marry her. He seemed to enjoy skirting around the subject, playing games.

'Do you know what I think?' she said suddenly as she decided to change tack. 'I think you are a man who takes his responsibilities seriously. You love Poppy and want to do the best for her...but deep down you are afraid of committing yourself to Jody.'

'Why is that?' He merely looked amused at the statement.

She shrugged. 'Because you are afraid of losing her the way you lost your wife. So your protective instinct is to back away from deep involvement.'

It was a wild guess but for a moment she thought she had struck the truth. The amusement had faded from his face. His mouth slanted in a firm, derisive line. 'Do nannies go in for psychology these days, then?'

'I'm right, aren't I?' she asked quietly.

'No, you are way off line.' He sounded annoyed. 'You are also way out of order. My relationship with Jody is none of your business. You are here to look after Poppy, not analyse my affairs.'

The sudden coolness in the air was almost palpable. Cathy felt as if he had just slapped her across the face. 'Well, pardon me,' she said frostily, 'but you haven't been averse to asking me a few personal questions. And you were well out of order this afternoon when you kissed me, weren't you?'

'Touché.' His voice was low. 'Maybe this should be a lesson to both of us to keep our respective distances.'

'If you say so.' She stood up and started to clear the empty dishes from the table, her movements brisk, angry.

Why was she angry? she wondered as she hurried

through to the kitchen. Pearce had every right to tell her
to mind her own business. She was prying.

She was also in some confused way getting emotionally involved here, she acknowledged reluctantly. She
had enjoyed Pearce's flirtatious manner earlier. The return to bussinesslike disdain had been a shock. She was
here to get a story, she reminded herself sharply. Her
job was the most important thing—nothing else should
influence her. No emotions should be coming into the
scenario.

She started to load the dishwasher, her movements
brisk. She was furious with herself.

'I've made you angry.' Pearce's voice made her look
around. He was leaning indolently against the doorframe, just watching her.

'No, I think I made you angry.'

He smiled. 'Let's not argue about it.'

His smile made Cathy feel defenceless and vulnerable.
She didn't want to feel attracted to him, but she was.
Given the circumstances, it was a mistake of vast pro-
portions.

'No, let's not.' She turned away from him to switch
the dishwasher on. 'We are probably both overtired from
our disturbed night.'

'Probably.' He sounded about as convinced as she felt.

Despite the polite conversation, there was a tense undercurrent in the air. Cathy could feel it twisting between
them like a serpent ready to bite.

'Would you like coffee?' she asked brightly as she
picked the kettle up.

'Did you remember to close the gates when Henri
went home?' The sudden question, asked in a very serious tone, made her frown and glance at him. He was
standing looking at the security monitors, a look of grim
displeasure on his face.

'Of course I did. I—' She broke off as she realised

that although she had closed the gates after Henri, she had forgotten to close them after the delivery of food.

He watched as her face flooded with incriminating colour. 'Honestly, Catherine! We could have a whole damn parade of reporters walking around here, not to mention burglars.'

She turned away, exasperated at such a folly. She had been so damned hassled with dinner that the gates had been the last thing on her mind. 'Well, I can't think of everything,' she muttered crossly.

She filled the kettle. Then stood with her back to Pearce, her eyes sightlessly fixed on the window as she waited for it to boil.

Knowing Pearce, the reporters would be less welcome than the burglars— Her thoughts broke off in horror as she saw a face pressed against the darkness of the window pane.

She couldn't see the features clearly because of the reflection of light on the glass. She could just see the pink of his skin and dark staring eyes. The shock was so intense that she stepped back and screamed piercingly.

'What the hell is it?' Pearce was at her side in a moment. 'What's wrong?' He gripped her arm, a look of deep concern on his face as he saw how pale she was and that she was shaking.

'There was somebody outside.' Her voice was very unsteady. 'Somebody was looking through the window at us.'

Pearce glanced up, but there was no one there. 'I'll ring through to my security firm,' he murmured, reaching for the phone.

He got through and gave a code number, before putting down the receiver again. Then he moved resolutely towards the back door.

'Don't go out there.' Cathy's voice was sharp with

anxiety. 'He could be armed and dangerous, just waiting for you.'

'I should think that after the way you screamed he will be miles away by now.'

Pearce grinned at her, but she wasn't amused. 'Even so...don't open the door, Pearce.' She reached out and took hold of his arm. 'I couldn't bear it if something happened to you. It would be all my fault for leaving the gates open and—'

'Come on, Catherine, calm down.' He turned towards her. 'It's OK, I won't open the door, not if you don't want me to.' His voice was soothing and she leaned her head against his chest.

'It's all my fault.' She bit down on her lip. 'I'm sorry I forgot the gates, Pearce...I was just so involved with dinner.' She leaned closer and his arms went around her.

'There's no real harm done...except, that is, to your nervous system.'

His voice sounded deep and warm. The faint scent of his cologne invaded her senses, reminding her of his dressing-gown and last night.

Suddenly she realised that she had moved into his arms and shock transformed into intense physical awareness.

'Do you feel better now?' he asked gently.

She pulled away slightly so that she could look up at him. It was a mistake. She felt as if she were drowning in his eyes.

'I feel wonderful when I'm in your arms.' She whispered the words huskily. The sentiment came straight from her heart, spoken without embarrassment, without deep reflection.

'Hell, Catherine!' His voice grated with a mixture of impatience and desire. She heard the two emotions clearly and her heart twisted. This wasn't a good idea. She knew it; he probably knew it. Even so, he bent his head and kissed her, and she responded. This was no gentle persuasion—it was fiercely passionate.

The touch of his lips against hers sent fires of delight racing through her. She pressed her body closer to his, wanting more. She couldn't think straight—all she could do was ride with the moment.

His hands were warm against her body, stroking down the slender curve of her waist.

The sound of the doorbell was what drew them apart.

Cathy stared up at him wordlessly, her eyes wide and filled with amazement at the strength of desire that had just flowed between them.

'So much for keeping our distance.' His voice was husky, betraying the fact that he was as stunned by what had just happened as she was.

The doorbell rang again.

'That will be the security people. I'd better let them in before they wake Poppy.'

She watched as he walked through to the hall. She had to leave here, she thought dazedly. Had to walk away before everything got out of control.

CHAPTER SEVEN

CATHY lay awake in her bed. The security men had been searching the grounds for ages. She had watched from her bedroom window as the heavy beams of torchlight slanted through the darkness. Then she had turned away to get her suitcase out from the wardrobe.

She had packed nothing. The case lay open and empty on the floor. Her eyes moved to it now. The sensible thing would be to leave. She had enough information to write a story of sorts. She knew that Pearce had been married before...she knew that he missed his wife deeply. It would suffice for a short column.

The trouble was that she didn't want to write the story, nor did she want to leave.

She was totally confused by her feelings. All she knew for sure at that moment was that she was as frightened as hell of her own emotions.

Never had she felt so drawn to someone as she was to Pearce. Even David, to whom she had been engaged for four short months, had never made her feel like this. Never had she felt such a powerful desire that obliterated all rational thought. She had wanted to melt into Pearce. She had wanted...and wanted... Her cheeks burned again at the memory.

There was a knock at her door and she sat up in her bed and wrapped her dressing-gown firmly around herself, shivering with sudden apprehension.

'Catherine, is it all right if I come in?' Pearce's voice was low in deference to the sleeping child in the nursery.

Cathy was silent for a moment. She reached for a tissue on the table next to her and dabbed at her eyes.

'Catherine?' He opened the door a fraction and looked around.

'I don't think your presence in here is such a good idea.' Her voice was low and uneven.

'Probably not.' He came further into the room. He was carrying a glass of brandy which he put down on the bedside table. 'I thought maybe you could use this,' he said softly.

'Thanks. But I don't like brandy.' She didn't look up at him—she couldn't bring herself to meet his eyes.

'Doesn't matter, It was an excuse to come in and see you, anyway.'

The honesty of his answer made her feel incredibly tense.

'Can I sit down?'

She nodded, thinking that he would pull the bedroom chair over, but instead he sat next to her on the edge of the bed.

'Did the security people find whoever was outside?' It was a brave attempt at rational conversation. She was fiercely aware of him. Even where his sleeve brushed against her arm her nerve-endings seemed to tingle.

'No. The grounds around here are massive. Hopefully, he'll be long gone by now.' He paused, then asked heavily, 'Do you want me to put your suitcase away for you?'

She glanced up and saw that he was looking at her open case.

'I was in the process of packing,' she told him with a sigh.

'You've only just unpacked.' His voice held a tinge of humour which, for some reason, really annoyed her.

'Well, what do you suggest I do?' She glared up at him. 'I can't stay here, can I? Not with this…this attraction that seems to have sprung up between us.'

'But I don't want you to go.'

She looked at him then, uncertain. 'You'll find someone else to look after Poppy.' She was aware of the regret in her voice, in her very soul. Ridiculous, but she had liked looking after Poppy...she loved being here.

His eyes moved over the pallor of her skin, the long heavy length of her blonde hair. 'Yes, but I want you.'

The words sent a hot sweep of confusion and desire through her. 'I...I hope you mean that in a business sense?'

'Do you?'

The quietly asked question made her eyes lock with his. Her heart felt as if it didn't belong to her. It was racing and she felt breathless, dizzy.

'I warned you earlier that I found you attractive.' He murmured the words almost to himself. 'And I know it's damn crazy. You are working for me. I'm in a position of trust having you here under my roof.'

The words 'position of trust' echoed inside her head. She was flagrantly abusing his trust in her. She was a fraud...he would despise her if he but knew.

'You mean I might scream sexual harassment if you were to kiss me again?' Her lips twisted drily. 'Like you, Pearce, I know this is crazy. I think it's best that I should leave.'

'Maybe you're right.' His voice was husky. 'So shall we say that you are formally handing in your notice to quit?'

She stared at him, her eyes wide. She had wanted him to argue the point, she realised. Her disappointment was acute and at the same time she was berating herself for being so stupid.

He touched the side of her face in a whisper-soft caress. 'Maybe if you weren't working for me I might not feel so damn guilty about kissing you again...and I want so much to kiss you again.'

Her breath caught painfully in her chest. He was very

close to her. She could feel his breath against her face. She wanted him to kiss her, the need like an ache deep inside. She tried desperately to fight it, to think sensibly.

'And what about Jody...?' Her voice was trembling with emotion. She was hanging onto control by a thread. 'Won't you feel guilty about cheating on her?'

He didn't answer for a moment, then his lips curved in a smile. 'We'll talk about Jody later.'

His voice held no guilt, just a positive deep sensuality that made her insides twist into tightly squeezed knots of desire. His lips moved closer to hers and she closed her eyes, feeling her body's traitorous need for him and unable to pull herself back from it.

His lips were addictively soft at first, then hungry with intensity. She felt as if a fierce undercurrent were tugging her away from the shores of sanity. Tugging, pulling unmercifully, until it was easier to give herself up to it.

She was in love with this man. The sudden realisation was awesome. It completely swamped her.

The kiss deepened. Pearce was a practised lover. He drew her further and further into a spiral of sensuality that was totally unlike anything she had ever known.

The covers of the bed were thrown back. His hands moved down over the curves of her body, feeling the naked softness of her breasts beneath the silk material of her dressing-gown, then stroked down over the taut flatness of her stomach and the gentle curve of her hips.

She was hazily aware that she was now lying back against the pillows of the bed, her arms wound around his shoulders and her hands stroking through the thick darkness of his hair.

She was out of control, hungry for him, when he pulled away from her.

'Don't stop.' Her eyes were wide as they sought and held his.

He reached out a hand and pulled it through the long honey-gold hair. 'You know that if I don't stop now...I might not be able to stop at all.' His voice was a deep murmur of sensuality. It made her heart race; it made her body glow with the most outrageously demanding needs.

She reached up and touched his face. It was a mute invitation that was echoed in her eyes.

The forceful, attractive features gave no hint of gentleness now, just desire—and it was a powerful play of emotion.

Her hair was like a golden cloud against the dark silk covers of the bed, her eyes the colour of emeralds as they met with the darkness of his. 'You do want me?' For the briefest moment doubt crept in. She wanted reassurance; she wanted to know if he had any deep feelings for her.

He said nothing, just slowly, deliberately, untied the belt of her dressing-gown, blatantly exposing the soft, naked contours of her body to his eyes.

She swallowed hard as he bent his head and kissed one rosy erect nipple.

'You are a very beautiful woman, Catherine.' His words were slurred with desire as he sat back from her, his hands covering her breasts and feeling their heaviness—caressing them, teasing them, until she shuddered with desire.

Then he kissed her and she responded with a fiery need that pulled away the last vestige of sanity.

His lips trailed a sweet path down the slender column of her neck over her breast. His hand moved from her waist towards her inner thigh, stroking her, teasing her so that she ached for him to move further up towards the soft core of her womanhood. When he did she moaned with abandonment.

He stopped to take off his clothes. The blue shirt, the jeans were quickly discarded and her eyes devoured his naked body greedily.

His skin had a satin golden tan. The powerful shoulders narrowed to his waist and slim hips.

As her eyes moved lower he laughed. 'You see, there is no doubt that I do want you.'

'No doubt,' she whispered, a soft tremor in her voice.

'Now all we need are contraceptives.'

She watched as he stretched out a hand to take some from the pocket of his jeans.

The fact that he had come in here prepared to make love to her struck her like a cool shower in summer.

She didn't blame him as such; after all, she had practically thrown herself at him downstairs. But even so it made her think. She didn't want to be used. She had never in her life gone in for casual sex and she didn't want to start now.

How could they have any kind of relationship when she had lied to him about who she was...and when he was involved with another woman?

Reality crashed around her. This wasn't right.

'Pearce...I think maybe this is a mistake.' Her voice was panicky as he rejoined her on the bed.

'Taking precautions is never a mistake,' he assured her, completely misunderstanding what she was saying. He bent his head and kissed her nipples, first one then the other, sucking her—tasting her. The ecstasy was pure and unrelenting as his hands stroked her body, sending waves of desire shooting through her and making her brain cloud with longing.

Then his hands moved to stroke between her legs and his lips trailed downwards to join them.

'Pearce, you had better stop.' It was the faintest murmur of protest and her body traitorously said something quite different. It responded absolutely, her need for him intense.

Her fingers clenched against the silk covers and with a supreme effort of willpower she forced herself to move away from him. 'Pearce, this isn't right.'

'Why isn't it?' His eyes were narrowed, watchful.

'I…I don't know.' She reached for her dressing-gown, clumsily draping it around her. 'It just doesn't feel right.'

'It felt pretty good to me.' He sat up and raked an impatient hand through his dark hair. Cathy could tell that he was fighting for control of his senses. There was a spark of anger in his eyes and she couldn't blame him for it.

She shivered. She felt angry as well, furious, in fact, that she had allowed herself to get into this situation.

She looked across at him and her heart twisted. She had fallen for him but how it had happened she didn't know. All she knew was that she loved him with every fibre of her soul.

She needed to tell him the truth about herself. Her article for the paper was unimportant, compared with the depth of feeling inside her.

If she told him now what would his reaction be? she wondered. Obviously he would be livid to begin with, but whether he would forgive her or not was down to how much he felt for her.

He was watching her silently and she knew that her confusion, her indecision, was there for him to see.

'Are you and Jody Sterling in love with each other?' She mumbled the question, feeling embarrassed and inadequate. Pearce had every right to shout at her—to call her a tease, she thought dismally.

His features darkened.

'Please try to understand, Pearce.' Her voice had risen

and almost simultaneously Poppy started to cry in the next room.

Cathy fumbled to get her dressing-gown on correctly and belt it. Her voice was low and pleading now. 'I need to know... I've never...ever...in my life gone in for casual relationships and I feel that if you and Jody are serious then perhaps it is only fair that you tell me up front.'

Pearce was dressing as she spoke. He flicked her a vaguely contemptuous look. 'I think we should discuss this in the cool light of morning,' he said disdainfully.

Cathy flinched. She had expected his anger, but not this coldness. He was looking at her as if she was beneath contempt.

'Pearce, I—'

Poppy's wail grew louder and she broke off and shook her head. 'I'd better see to her—'

'Oh, no.' He put a hand on her shoulder. 'I'll see to her. You've given in your notice...remember?'

With that, he strode out of the room.

CHAPTER EIGHT

EARLY morning sunlight streamed into Cathy's bedroom as she dressed in a casual short skirt and top.

She was tired. It was hardly surprising as she hadn't slept at all last night and not much the night before either.

She brushed her hair and stared at her reflection in the mirror. Her eyes were shadowed, her skin pale. For hours she had lain awake last night, practising what she should have said to Pearce—going over and over the situation until she had felt sick with it.

She sighed and put down her hair-brush to wander through to the nursery. Poppy was not in her cot. Cathy stared down at the ruffled, lace-trimmed blanket and felt tears welling up inside her.

She had listened to Poppy's cries last night, had heard Pearce murmuring soft endearments to her as he'd tried to settle the baby down. She had ached to come out to them, but she hadn't dared to face Pearce.

It was only when the nursery was silent that she had risked tiptoeing in to check on the child.

She had stopped just inside the door when she had noticed Pearce, sitting on the settee by the window.

At first she had thought that he was awake and then, as she'd advanced further into the room, she had seen that he had fallen asleep, his head resting against the side cushion and his arms folded protectively over a sleeping Poppy.

Cathy had stood transfixed for a few moments, watching the sleeping man. His features were gentle in sleep, a lock of dark hair falling across his forehead.

The urge to go across and touch him, run her fingers through his hair and whisper how much she loved him, had been intense. Instead, she had returned to her bedroom, and despite the heat of the night she had felt cold with loneliness...with longing.

The memory of those feelings returned now as she crept quietly down the stairs. She didn't know what she was going to say to Pearce this morning...how she should deal with what had happened last night. She was in some way frightened of facing him.

As she went silently down the corridor towards the kitchen she heard his voice. At first she thought that he was talking to Poppy, but then she hesitated as she heard the name Jody mentioned.

She paused with her hand on the doorhandle of the kitchen. The door was open slightly and she could see Pearce, standing with his back to her. He was talking on the phone and with his other hand he was trying to spoon-feed Poppy her breakfast.

'So, how are you?' he was saying. His voice was warm, filled with concern.

'Of course I've been worried about you. Poppy has been missing you like crazy too...' There was silence, then he laughed. 'OK, I'll give her a big kiss from Mummy and tell her you are coming home soon.'

Cathy's heart squeezed painfully. She had her answer. Pearce was in love with Jody, no matter what he had said about not marrying her.

She was relieved in one way. She had made the right decision, calling a halt to things last night. Then, at the same time, she felt incredibly hurt. How could he have kissed her so passionately when he had such feeling for Jody? She felt suddenly that she would never understand men.

For an awful blinding moment she remembered her fiancé David. He had told her that he loved her, had

made promises of undying love. The pain of finding out
that he had been having an affair with another woman
was engraved deep inside her. She had got over David
a long time ago, but the lesson burnt vividly.

Why she had lowered her defence barriers for Pearce
Tyrone was a complete mystery. She had known him a
few days…and had fallen for him almost on sight. It
was out of character…it was appallingly naïve. He had
made no promises to her—no declaration of love—and
yet she had offered herself freely to him last night in a
way that had been almost wanton.

She made a movement and Pearce turned and caught
sight of her.

'I've got to go, Jody. I'll see you at the weekend,
then? Hopefully the strike will be over. OK, me too.'
He laughed at something she said and put down the receiver.

'Good morning, Catherine.' He sounded bright, no
trace in his voice of the coolness of last night.

'Good morning.' She came further into the room, trying to avoid his eyes. 'Hello, sweetheart,' she said to
Poppy.

The little girl smiled up at her. She had a dimple in
her chin, Cathy noticed suddenly. Why that should make
a wedge of affection and sadness well up inside her she
didn't know. She had to turn away. She poured herself
coffee from the pot on the counter, taking her time with
the task in order to get her wayward emotions back in
check.

When she sat back at the table Pearce remarked suddenly, 'You look tired.'

She glanced across at him. In contrast to her, he
looked remarkably fresh. The interrupted night's sleep
and the hours in the nursery seemed never to have happened.

'I am a little,' she admitted grudgingly.

'I'm not surprised really.' The sympathy in his tone made her emotions clench. She didn't want him to be nice to her...she might cry.

'I've decided we should take the day off today. Go out and relax.'

She frowned at him. 'How can I take the day off when I've stopped working for you?' Her voice held more than a trace of bitter sarcasm.

'No, you haven't.' He met her eyes steadily. 'For me to take your leaving seriously you would have to give me written notice.'

'Pearce, I don't know what your game is but—' She started to back away from the situation.

'No games.' He leaned across and touched her face. It was a fleeting gesture of tenderness but it made every sensitive nerve-ending in her body flare into life. 'I really just don't want you to go, Catherine.'

The confusion of longing and wariness his husky words stirred up made her feel so incredibly vulnerable that she could barely speak for fear of just breaking down. 'The thing is that you are in love with Jody, Pearce, and I—'

'No, the thing is that we need to talk about our feelings. We need to discuss last night and I need to tell you about Jody and me.'

She stared at him, her heart beating erratically. 'So, tell me,' she invited softly, her eyes wide and glimmering.

He smiled, as if in some way her reply satisfied him. 'Later.' He got up from his chair. 'We'll go out for the day, just you, me and Poppy.'

'But, Pearce, I—'

'See to Poppy, will you? Make sure she has a sun-hat and sun-cream and a change of clothing, and so on.' He moved briskly towards the door. 'Oh, and don't forget to put your own sun-cream and swimsuit in the bag.'

The engine of the boat stopped and Pearce dropped anchor. There was silence, except for the gentle lap of water against the sides of the luxury yacht.

Cathy looked out across the water. It was a perfect day. The sky was a blazing cobalt blue. They were a couple of miles off shore from Villefranche, a picturesque little village perched on the side of a mountain. Cathy drank in the scenery. The vibrant yellow, pink and red brick houses, packed against the hill, looked like a glorious abstract painting.

She breathed in the tangy salt air and relaxed against the rail of the boat, feeling the heat of the sun invade her body. If there had been just her and Pearce and no complications this would indeed be heaven, she thought sadly.

Pearce came down the steps from the bridge. He had taken off his T-shirt and was just wearing a pair of navy blue shorts. 'Hot, isn't it?' he remarked. 'Would you like a swim before lunch?'

She tried not to look at his chest but flicked a glance through the sliding glass door towards Poppy, who was in a play-pen in the air-conditioned cool of the lounge.

'We'll take it in turns,' Pearce said. 'I'll keep watch over Poppy while you are in the water and vice versa.'

She nodded and turned to go down to the cabins. She had her bikini on underneath her white shorts and T-shirt and she could have stripped off next to him. However, she felt too embarrassed to do that.

Her lips twisted wryly at her own foolishness. Pearce had seen every part of her anatomy last night and yet today she was modestly retiring inside in case he watched her undress. It seemed symbolic somehow of the whole morning. Since they had set out they had been treating each other with a kind of polite wariness.

It took just a couple of seconds to discard her clothes and then go up to dive into the cool, refreshing water of the Mediterranean. After the heat of the midday sun it was a fabulous feeling.

She swam a fair distance from the yacht and then looked back at it.

It was a lovely ship, long and sleek, with masts that towered into the sky. Because it was such a still day the sails were down and they had relied on the engines. She could imagine how impressive the ship would look when in full sail.

When Pearce had said that he would take her out for the day she had had no idea that he'd meant on his yacht.

At the very bottom of Pearce's estate he had his own private mooring for the luxury vessel. He also had a large ivy-covered boathouse on the water's edge in which he kept *The Siren* when she wasn't in use.

He had grinned when he had noticed Cathy's look of surprise. 'This way we can be quite alone,' he had said softly. 'No reporters to bother us. Just you and me—and Poppy, of course.'

The words echoed in her mind now. 'No reporters to bother us.' If he but knew. She turned back towards the ship, swimming powerfully through the water—hoping that the exercise would help clear her mind.

From the way Pearce had spoken before they left she had thought he wanted to be alone with her, wanted to talk, yet he had made no attempt to do so. When she had tried to bring up the subject of Jody Sterling a little while before he had abruptly changed the subject. The only thing that she could think of was that he was plagued by conscience. That he did desire her, but desire was overshadowed by the reality of the fact that he loved Jody.

'How was the water?' Pearce asked as she pulled herself back on deck.

'Exhilarating.' She gave him a strained smile and reached for her towel which he was holding.

He didn't give it to her. 'I don't think I'm going to allow you to cover yourself up. You look too damn good.'

'Don't be silly, Pearce.' She tried to take it from him but he snatched it away, a gleam of teasing humour on his attractive face as his eyes moved with slow deliberation over her figure.

She could feel her body knotting with sensual tension at the look on his face. Her breasts felt taut, the nipples sensitive and raised, and it had nothing to do with the cool water she had just plunged into.

'Give it to me, Pearce,' she pleaded, a catch in her voice.

'I thought you would never ask.' With one sure movement he took her into his arms and kissed her.

Slowly sensuous, deliberately taunting, he kissed her with a skill that made her feel totally helpless, a prisoner of desire. She responded instantly with a deep yearning. She wanted more. She had no willpower where he was concerned, none at all.

She pushed away from him as Poppy made fretful little murmurs.

'I had better see to her,' she said breathlessly, but there was also a spark of anger in her voice. She was angry at herself for succumbing so easily to his advances. It was starting to occur to her that Pearce was only interested in her body. That he had invited her out here not to talk to her, but to seduce her. The notion hurt unbearably.

'Catherine.' He caught her by the arm as she made to move past him.

She looked down at his hand on her arm with an expression of fury. 'Poppy will be hungry. I think our little dalliance can wait...don't you?'

She knew that the barbed comment had hit home

when she looked up and saw annoyance darken his handsome features, then he shrugged. 'If you say so.'

She watched as he went across the deck to dive cleanly into the sea. Only then did she let out her breath in a shuddering sigh.

She couldn't think straight anywhere near Pearce. Her mind was clouded with emotions that stunned her... frightened her.

She towelled herself dry briskly and put her clothes back on.

Perhaps she shouldn't have snapped at him like that. To be fair to him, she was jumping to conclusions that he had invited her out here today just to seduce her. Maybe his intentions were honourable. He could just be waiting for the right moment to talk to her.

The memory of his phone call to Jody this morning cut across that thought. He had sounded so warm, so tender when he had spoken to the other woman. The pain she felt at that memory spilled inside her. Suddenly it seemed most likely that Pearce had wanted her out here to finish what they had started last night. Then he would calmly wave goodbye to her before Jody came home.

She had once asked him if he was a womaniser and now she had her answer. She had to keep that fact to the front of her mind and she had to bow out of this situation quickly.

Poppy gave a small cry of discontent and she turned to attend to her.

'Yes, I know you're hungry, little one,' she murmured gently to the child. For a moment her eyes moved over the baby.

Poppy had wound her way around her heart—just as Pearce had done. Pearce and Poppy—what a fatal combination. She would miss them both terribly. Once she had written her story she would never, ever, see them again, that was certain.

She turned towards the cupboards in the galley and busied herself with Poppy's lunch. She wasn't in love with Pearce, she told herself sharply in denial of the raw feeling of hurt inside. It was infatuation, nothing more. She would get over Pearce in a matter of days.

The idea made her feel a little better as she went about her work.

She had finished feeding Poppy, and the child was sitting happily in her high chair drinking some fruit juice from her bottle, when Pearce came back.

He had changed into a white shirt and white shorts which emphasised the golden tan of his body, the darkness of his hair.

She tried not to pay too much attention to how he looked, tried to act as if she wasn't aware of everything about him. 'Did you enjoy your swim?' she asked brightly.

'Well, it cooled me down.' His tone was deep, with an irony she chose to ignore.

'It's just salad for lunch I'm afraid. I—'

She broke off as he caught hold of her arm. 'You know I couldn't really give a damn about lunch.'

'Is this the same man who told me he was very particular about meals?' Desperately she tried to lighten the mood.

For a moment his lips slanted in a wryly amused way. 'I'm beginning to wonder that myself,' he murmured huskily.

'Pearce, please...' Her protest was no more than a whisper as he leaned closer and kissed her.

She responded instantly to the soft, inviting pressure of his lips.

'Please what?' he murmured as he pulled back. 'Please stop? Please don't stop?'

She hardly knew the answer to that herself. 'I...' She drew in a long shuddering breath. 'I'm trying to be sensible...trying to think clearly.'

'Would it make a difference if I told you that Jody Sterling and I are not having an affair?' he asked huskily.

She frowned. 'You mean you've finished with her?'

'I didn't say that.'

'She's finished with you?' Incredulity was clear in her voice. She couldn't imagine any woman rejecting Pearce.

'Let's just say we are not an item.'

A shiver of ecstasy and hope flickered through her but she pushed it away and with it she pushed him away. Her eyes narrowed warily on his handsome face. 'I don't believe you.'

'Believe it or not, it's the truth,' he said firmly.

Cathy stared at him. The need to believe him was intense, but suspicion wouldn't go away. She kept remembering the conversation she had overheard this morning. He had sounded so tender and caring. 'You're not going to tell me that you have some kind of open relationship with her, are you?'

'No, Catherine.' His voice was starting to grow impatient. 'But Jody does go her way and I go mine.'

'I bet you didn't mention our little dalliance to her when you phoned her this morning.'

It was a question she hadn't meant to ask and she was furious with herself the moment it was spoken, especially when he replied calmly, 'Catherine, you have no need to be jealous of Jody, I can assure you.'

'I'm not jealous.' She shrugged airily, her voice overly cheerful. 'Why should I be jealous? Last night was a mistake. Passion overtook common sense. Let's leave it there and try to put things back to a proper footing.'

'Do you really think we can?'

Her eyes veered away from him. 'No.' She acknowledged the truth reluctantly. 'But we should try. What else can we do?'

'I know what I'd like to do.'

The blatantly sexy way he spoke those words made her skin flush with heat. 'You mean you want to take me to bed,' she said in a brittle tone. 'Don't you think that's just going to make everything worse?'

'I think it would make me feel a hell of a lot better.'

She looked at him then, her eyes narrowed. 'You know I once thought I was in love with a man who was a lot like you.'

Pearce didn't seem put out by her contemptuous tone. 'Is that a fact?'

'He told me that I was the most wonderful thing to have happened to him, that he loved me more than anything else in the whole world. Then I discovered that he was saying exactly the same thing to some other woman.' Just thinking about David Collins made Cathy feel angry. She fixed Pearce with a look of disdain. 'So, you see, Jody Sterling has my complete sympathy.'

'I presume you are talking about your ex-fiancé.' Pearce shrugged. 'And I don't think he sounds anything like me. I have never had to resort to telling a woman I loved her to get her into bed.'

'And the moon is made of cheese,' she grated sarcastically and made to turn away.

He caught hold of her arm. 'Well, I didn't whisper any words of love to you last night,' he grated harshly. 'Is that where I went wrong?'

For a stunned second she couldn't believe what he had said. Then her hand came up and she slapped him hard across the side of his face.

She didn't wait to see his reaction but turned and raced out towards the deck.

Heat hit her as she stepped from the air-conditioned galley. She was shaking with reaction, regretting what she had done whilst at the same time thinking how much Pearce had deserved it.

He caught up with her before she had taken many steps. Catching hold of her arm, he swung her around to face him.

The anger on his face made her rethink the advisability of that last move. Perhaps she shouldn't have lashed out quite so violently. 'Before you say anything, I apologise,' she said quickly.

'Damn right you're apologising,' he rasped harshly.

'Come on, Pearce, you sounded so damned conceited. It made me furious.'

'Why, exactly? Because I reminded you that I didn't tell you I loved you last night?'

'Don't be ridiculous. I didn't expect you to say anything of the sort.' She looked up at him, her eyes wide and anxious. 'Last night I just...well, I just got cold feet, for want of a better explanation.' She swallowed hard. 'I've never gone in for casual sex.' She spoke in a low trembling tone. 'I didn't, however, expect declarations of undying love... I just wanted to know where I stood. How you felt about Jody.'

'I've told you.' he said staunchly.

'What exactly?' She glared at him. 'You've told me very little, Pearce.'

'And you want to know all the grim details?' The quietly asked question made her senses reel. There was something about his tone of voice...something about the watchful look in his eyes.

Cathy had the strangest feeling that she was being toyed with...played with like some doll. Perhaps it was her journalist's instinct, perhaps it was feminine intuition. But she had the sudden, clearest feeling that all wasn't as it seemed.

She frowned, trying to make sense of the idea...trying to grasp the obscure notion and clarify exactly what it was...but it slipped elusively away.

Silence stretched between them, a tense silence filled with emotion.

The sound of an engine drifted in the salt air, penetrating hazily through Cathy's consciousness. It wasn't until Pearce pulled away from her that she heard it clearly. It was a boat engine and a woman's voice calling.

'Ahoy there.' Her singsong voice carried across the water.

'And I said we were going have some peace and quiet,' Pearce remarked as he leaned against the rail of the boat and looked down.

A small cabin cruiser drew alongside and dropped anchor. Cathy followed Pearce to the rail.

'Permission to come aboard, Captain,' A woman in a very skimpy red bikini was laughing across at Pearce, her dark hair swinging in a shining bob as she waved her hands up in the air to get his attention. It took a few moments for Cathy to recognise her.

'Laura, this is a surprise.' An expression of lazy amusement crossed Pearce's handsome features. 'Come aboard, by all means.'

Laura Houston wasted no time in complying with the invitation. Cathy felt a dart of disappointment at the intrusion, but it was nothing to the shock she felt when she noticed that Laura wasn't on her own.

Behind the woman, a camera strung casually around his neck, was David Collins.

As their eyes met he lifted his hand in a small salute, a laughing gleam in his eyes.

CHAPTER NINE

'AND this is my friend, David Collins,' Laura said, her tone gushing.

Cathy cringed as David stepped forward to shake hands with Pearce, his manner politely courteous.

Her whole body felt as if it were on fire. She was so furious that she could hardly keep still. What the hell was David Collins doing here?

'And this is Poppy's nanny...' Laura frowned. 'I'm really sorry,' she said to Cathy, 'but I can't remember your name.'

'Cathy Fielding.' Cathy's voice was icy, in sharp contrast to the hot fury inside. It was an almighty effort to extend her hand to meet with David's.

'Very pleased to meet you, Cathy.' There was an amused, mocking expression in his eyes as he took her hand. He held it for just a moment longer than was necessary and she pulled away with a sharply instinctive movement.

'Would anyone care for a drink?' Pearce asked politely as he led the way across to the sun-chairs, positioned near the bow of the boat.

'A glass of wine would be lovely.' Laura moved one of the chairs from the shade so that she could sit fully in the warmth of the sun.

Cathy stood awkwardly. She could hardly take her eyes off David. She was so shocked to see him like this. What the hell was he doing here? He couldn't possibly be a real friend of Laura's. It was more likely that he had done some research and found Laura to be the easiest route to get to Pearce.

Cathy had worked with David enough times to know his style. He wasn't above using anyone or anything to get his story.

Her eyes moved over him thoughtfully. He hadn't changed at all in the last two years. It was like plunging back in time.

He was still incredibly good-looking. The same thick blond hair and lean athletic figure that had always turned women's heads. He was wearing shorts that closely fitted his slender hips and a dark-coloured T-shirt. The blatantly professional camera strung casually across his broad chest made her pulse race. The man had a cool nerve.

'Catherine?'

Suddenly she was aware that Pearce was speaking to her and she hadn't heard a word.

'Sorry?' She blinked and looked at him.

'I said, what would you like to drink?' he repeated patiently.

'Just a lemonade.' Her eyes veered back to David again and he grinned at her.

'So it's two beers, a wine and—'

'I'll get them, Pearce.' She cut across him. She needed to escape from this situation for a moment and gather herself together. 'I want to check on Poppy, anyway.'

Pearce shrugged and sat down. 'OK. Thanks.'

She was shaking when she went down into the galley. She should have told Pearce the truth about herself last night, she realised forcefully. Now David Collins was going to make everything unbearable.

She looked at Poppy who was still happily drinking her juice, her little toes kicking in baby-sweet contentedness.

'You're really getting into this nanny routine.' David appeared behind her, making her jump. 'How are you, sweetheart?'

She turned to look at him coldly. 'Don't call me that,' she warned him unsteadily. 'And just what in the hell are you doing here?'

'I wondered the same thing yesterday afternoon when you drove past me in Pearce Tyrone's car,' he said laconically.

'So you were among the reporters at the gates!' She shook her head. 'I thought you were working in Germany these days.'

'I get around.' He smiled and started to come closer. 'It's been a long time, Cath. You're looking good.' His gaze travelled thoughtfully over her slender body.

She darted a frightened look up at the door in case Pearce came in. 'Cut the corn, David,' she snarled.

'I was being serious…two long years and here we are again.' He reached to touch her face and she flinched away from him.

'Don't touch me,' she told him in no uncertain voice. 'And what do you mean by "here we are again"?'

'Working together, of course. Thanks for leaving the gate open for me last night, by the way.'

Her heart slammed furiously against her chest. 'I didn't leave it open for you.' Her eyes narrowed suddenly. 'It was you at the window last night, wasn't it?'

He grinned. 'I must say it all looked very cosy.'

Her cheeks flooded with colour. 'How dare you spy on me like that!'

'Oh, cut the holier-than-thou routine.' David shook a finger at her. 'As soon as I saw you yesterday afternoon I made it my business to phone your paper and speak to Mike. He told me all about how you got in with Tyrone. I have to hand it to you, Cath…brilliant piece of deception. You haven't lost your touch.'

'As I recall, you were the one who was brilliant at deception,' Cathy replied coolly.

'Ow!' He gave her a reproachful look but, like every-

thing else about David Collins, it wasn't serious. 'I was
kind of hoping you were going to let bygones be bygones... It really would be the sensible thing to do—
now that we are partners again.'

'We are not partners in anything.' Cathy's voice rose
unsteadily. She felt as if she were in the middle of some
ghastly dream, that this couldn't possibly be happening.

'Well, Mike was absolutely delighted when I rang
him. Told me he was having a hell of a job getting a
good photographer out to help you.' His mouth slanted
in a wry smile. 'He more or less begged my professional
services. Told me to name my price.'

Anger thundered through Cathy, in wave after furious
wave. 'I wouldn't work with you if it was the only job
in the universe and my life hinged on it.'

'Don't be bitter, Cath, it doesn't suit you,' he said
nonchalantly. 'We are both professionals. What happened between us once should not influence us now.
Together we could put together a hell of a good story.
Surely that's what matters?'

Cathy's eyes narrowed. 'I'm not bitter,' she told him
assuredly. She had got over David ages ago and she
didn't want anything to do with him. 'But we are not
doing anything together. This is my story. I don't want
you or anyone else in my way.'

He ignored her completely. 'I got a good photograph
of Tyrone kissing you yesterday afternoon. What's the
angle?'

'The angle is that if you don't leave right now I'm
going to open up my mouth and I'm going to scream
bloody murder. Then Tyrone is going to race down here
and he will throw you bodily from his property, probably
bringing a few charges against you for trespassing while
he is at it.' She glared at him. 'How's that?'

David didn't look in the slightest bit worried. 'If you
do that then I will just have to tell him that you are also

trespassing...then he can throw us both off here to-gether.'

Cathy glared at him. 'You wouldn't dare.'

He lifted one eyebrow and fixed her with a look that said, try me.

'You always were impossible.'

'And you were always beautiful.' His eyes moved over her face. 'It's no wonder Tyrone let you into his house without too much of a fuss.'

'He thinks I'm a member of his staff.'

'He doesn't look at you like a member of staff. I've got some good close-ups to prove it.'

'You're crazy.' Cathy shook her head. 'Tyrone is in love with Jody Sterling.'

David's lips twisted ironically. 'Who is talking about love...? I was talking about sex. Jody Sterling isn't around, and you are a good-looking girl.'

'I don't like the way your mind works, David,' she told him in a brittle tone. 'And, tell me, how on earth do you know Laura?'

'A bit of detective work,' He smiled, looking pleased with himself. Then he glanced over at Poppy, who was watching them as if she understood what they were say-ing.

'And this is the much-talked-about Poppy, I take it?' He lifted his camera. 'Take that bottle from her mouth, will you, Cath? It spoils a good shot.'

'No, I won't.' Cathy had the craziest urge to put her-self between Poppy and the camera. She was disgusted with David...and then, bearing in mind that she herself had been taking photographs of Poppy a few days ago, she was disgusted with herself.

'I don't suppose Laura knows that you are a reporter?' She tried to distract his attention away from the baby.

'Don't be silly.' He laughed. 'So, how are you doing with the story? Got any juicy titbits yet?'

'If I had I certainly wouldn't tell you,' she said sharply.

'Now, don't be like that.' He frowned and turned his complete attention to her again. 'You either work with me on this or you don't work at all.'

'Is that a threat?' Her voice was cool.

'More of a promise.' He reached for the fridge and started to get some cans of beer out and then a bottle of wine. 'Don't mind if I make myself at home, do you?' he asked. 'But I told Pearce that I was coming down here to give you a hand. He might start wondering where we are if we don't go back up in a minute.'

'I don't care what he thinks,' Cathy told him firmly.

'Don't you?' David's head turned towards the door as they heard steps on the stairway. 'Well, if you don't care then here's your chance to tell him the truth.'

Cathy didn't have a chance to reply because Pearce walked into the room at that moment.

'Thought you had got lost, David,' he said easily, but behind the nonchalant manner Cathy sensed a watchfulness about him.

'I was just talking to your delightful young employee,' David said with a smile. Then he looked directly over at Cathy. 'You were just about to say something, Catherine?'

It was a blatant challenge. He was daring her to either speak up and tell Pearce everything now or agree to work with him.

Cathy gritted her teeth and glanced across at Pearce. If she told Pearce who David really was she had no doubt that David would reciprocate. Then they would both be thrown off the yacht.

'I...I was just saying that I'd made a light lunch. There should be enough to go around. Should I bring it up on deck?'

Pearce nodded. 'Good idea. Do you want me to give you a hand carrying anything?'

'No. I'll manage.'

'I'll carry Poppy up, then,' he said, lifting the baby from her chair. 'I think she could do with some fresh air.'

As they all turned to leave the room David flashed her a triumphant look behind Pearce's back.

Cathy's expression was cooly noncommittal. David may believe that he had just won a point, but Cathy had no intention of working with him. She had decided to wait until she had Pearce on his own and then tell him the whole sordid truth. Fling herself on his mercy and hope that he would find it in his heart to forgive her. It was the only option she had. She no longer cared about getting an article out of this...the only thing she cared about was Pearce.

For Cathy, lunch was a strained affair. She said very little, her gaze moving again and again to Pearce as she tried to imagine his reaction when she told him the truth.

She doubted that he would forgive her and the pain of that was intense. The only thing that was clear in her mind was that she loved him...all the denials she had tried to make earlier just seemed ludicrous now in the face of her fear and her uncertainty. She was definitely overboard about Pearce. Just when he had started to become important to her and her work here unimportant was hazy in her mind.

He looked across and met her eyes. A wave of longing swept over her. Longing and bitter-sweet regret. She looked away from him, hardly able to bear the feelings inside herself.

David, on the other hand, was positively brimming with confidence and seemed to be very much in his element.

'This is pure bliss, isn't it?' Laura remarked, reaching

for her glass of wine and holding her face up to the heat of the sun.

'Yes, I'd have to agree with you.' David leaned back in his sun-lounger. 'Ordinarily I don't like sailing. I get terribly sea-sick. But when the weather is like this…it is indeed bliss.'

'So, what do you do for a living, David?' Pearce asked as he poured the man another beer.

'David is in insurance.' Laura was the one to answer. 'He's on holiday here and actually we only met last night, at my party.'

'I gate-crashed.' David said solemnly. 'I only heard about it through a friend of a friend.'

'Well, it's not necessarily true that you gate-crashed, darling.' Laura patted his knee reassuringly. 'I invited everyone. And we had a super time. I told you that you should have come, Pearce.' There was a hint of reproach in the woman's voice and in the wide beautiful eyes that she turned on him.

For the first time it occurred to Cathy that Laura Houston was more than just attracted to Pearce. It seemed suddenly very obvious that she was trying to make him jealous.

'David didn't arrive until late, but he didn't go home until the early hours of the morning…did you, David?'

'We had a good time all right,' David agreed nonchalantly.

'Well, you both seem remarkably fresh, seeing you had a late night.' Pearce grinned.

If stirring jealousy had indeed been Laura's intention she seemed to have failed. Pearce didn't seem very worried.

'Oh, you know me, Pearce, I can party until dawn.' Laura slanted a look over at David. 'I thought we might do it all over again tonight.'

'Sounds good to me.' David smiled. 'How about if

we make it a foursome? We could go into Monte Carlo, have dinner and a few games at the casino.' He looked directly at Cathy. 'How about it, Catherine?'

'I can't go.' Cathy didn't even hesitate. She looked over at David pointedly. 'I'm here to look after Poppy.'

Annoyance was very clear on David's face for a moment. 'Surely you get a night off?'

'Not until the end of the week.' Cathy stood up in case Pearce might interrupt them and say that it was all right. She didn't want to go out in a foursome and she certainly didn't want to be anywhere around David. 'If you'll excuse me,' she said politely as she picked Poppy up from where Pearce had positioned her under the shade of a parasol, 'I think Poppy is ready for her afternoon sleep.'

'So, Pearce—' David turned his attention to the other man as Cathy walked away from them '—Poppy is your daughter, I take it?'

Cathy hesitated by the door and then smiled as Pearce said nonchalantly, 'She's the light of my life.'

All through lunch David had tried unsuccessfully to get the conversation onto personal lines and Pearce had fielded his comments with an ease that had made the other man become more and more direct in his questions.

Cathy hurried on down to the galley.

It wasn't easy getting Poppy to settle in her carrycot. The child seemed overtired and fretful.

'Come on, darling,' Cathy whispered gently. 'You are not missing anything out there, I can assure you.' She sat patiently rocking the cot, and the child's eyes kept closing then opening again as she tried to fight sleep.

The baby had just lost her battle and was fast asleep when David came down to join her.

She flicked a glance up at him and noticed that he looked disgruntled.

'What's the matter? Hasn't Pearce answered any of your questions yet?' She couldn't resist the sarcastic dig.

'You know damn well he hasn't,' he murmured with a frown.

'Maybe you're losing your touch?'

'Don't bet on it. I'll break through any time now.'

The confident words irritated Cathy. 'Well, go and do so, then,' she muttered angrily. 'And stop following me around like a puppy dog. 'Pearce is bound to get suspicious.'

'I don't see why. You are a very attractive girl.' David opened the fridge and took out another can of beer. 'Anyway, I told him I wanted a drink.'

'And you should watch how much you are drinking,' she told him disapprovingly. 'The more you drink the more careless you get with the things you say.'

'What's the matter? Frightened your boyfriend will be upset when he learns that you have been leading him on?'

'I haven't been leading him on and he's not my boyfriend.'

He shrugged. 'Maybe. Mike tells me that you are under orders to do whatever it takes to get a good story.'

Cathy was really outraged now. 'Are you suggesting that I'm trying to seduce Pearce just to get a story?'

'Oh don't go all moral on me, Cath. I know only too well how prim and proper and utterly virginal you like to keep yourself. No, I was referring to the way you didn't seem to complain about the way he kissed you yesterday afternoon. The way you looked at him across the dinner table last night. You are either smitten, or you are using your femininity like a mantrap.'

'Don't judge everyone by your own standards. You may be employing those tactics with Laura but I—'

'You are in no position to preach, Cath. You are in

Pearce's house under false pretences, no matter how you feel about it.'

Cathy stared at him. He was right, of course. She was in no position to lecture him on ethics.

'Anyway, you play the vamp, or whatever it is you are doing, and get all you can and I'll get some shots of you both. Then we can put the whole thing together.' He reached into the back of his camera case and held a small cassette recorder out to her. 'You'll need this. Mike said you wouldn't have one with you.'

Cathy looked at the instrument with distaste, but she took it from him. It was probably better just to pretend to go along with him. If she told him outright that she had no intention of working with him, no intention of recording anything Pearce said to her, he would probably cause a scene.

She pushed the recorder deep into her handbag and then turned towards the carry-cot as Poppy murmured in her sleep.

'You had better go back up on deck.' She lowered her voice to a whisper. 'Apart from the fact that you are annoying me like hell, you are going to wake Poppy up.'

'Don't worry, I'm going.' He patted his camera. 'I just want that photograph of Poppy first.'

'I'd rather you didn't take photographs on board my boat.'

Pearce's cool voice startled both of them.

He was standing in the open doorway, just watching them.

'Heavens, Pearce, you made me jump.' David was the first to gather himself together. 'I didn't hear you coming down the stairs.'

Cathy was nervously wondering how much he had heard of their conversation. It was hard to tell from the expression on his face. The dark features seemed shuttered somehow, impassive. She waited for him to say something—to order them both off his property.

'You don't really mind if I take a photograph, do you, Pearce?' David persisted. 'I'll send you a copy, if you like. It will be a happy memory to look back over on a cold rainy day.'

'We don't get many cold days in the South of France,' Pearce said easily. 'However, having said that, I've just come down to tell you that the weather seems to be changing. I think it might be wise if we head back to shore.'

Cathy started to relax. Judging from his manner, Pearce couldn't have heard anything very much.

David, on the other hand, looked worried for the first time since he had come aboard. 'Really?' He pulled a face and headed for the door. 'We are not going to have a storm, are we? I'm afraid I'm not a very good sailor out on choppy seas.'

'I don't think it will be anything much.' Pearce shrugged. 'The weather forecast was good before we set out.'

Cathy followed the men up onto deck. The sky was still a brilliant blue but a strong breeze was blowing in across the water, making the boat dance a little on the choppy waves.

'I don't feel very well,' David complained, leaning against the rail.

'Don't be silly, darling,' Laura laughed. It's just a little breeze. I bet you didn't even notice it before Pearce went down and told you.'

'Well no...but this is a big vessel.' David pointed at the small boat they had arrived in. 'I bet we'll feel it on her,' he said nervously. 'I think we should go before it gets worse.'

Cathy tried hard to suppress a smile of pleasure. She could hardly wait to get rid of David.

Laura put on a T-shirt over her bikini and then stood on tiptoe to kiss Pearce goodbye. 'I'll see you later, then?' There was a questioning look in her eyes. There was also an intimacy about the moment that made Cathy feel somehow as if she shouldn't be listening.

'Come for dinner tomorrow,' Pearce said gently.

She smiled and the shadow of sadness seemed to lift from her face. 'Eight o'clock?'

He nodded.

Cathy's heart beat uncomfortably. She stood next to Pearce and watched as David and Laura climbed down to their boat.

'Did that invitation include David?' Cathy felt compelled to ask the question, even though she probably shouldn't have drawn attention to the fact that she had been listening in to his conversation.

'I don't think she will bring David...do you?' He turned to look at her.

Something about his expression, his voice, made her hesitate. 'Well...no.'

'Are you disappointed?'

Confusion raced through her. 'Disappointed that you have invited Laura to dinner, or disappointed that David won't be coming...which do you mean?'

He smiled, his manner infuriatingly laconic. 'Either will do.'

She glared at him. 'It's none of my business who you choose to invite to your house...is it? And as for David...' She hesitated briefly. 'To be honest, I don't really like him.'

'Is that so?' One dark eyebrow lifted sardonically. 'He seemed to like you.'

Her heart missed a beat. She had seen Pearce in a lot of different moods over these last few days, but somehow she couldn't work this one out.

He waved as Laura pulled her boat away, then turned

back to her. 'Anyway, I invited Laura for dinner so we could discuss some business. Now, how about a drink?'

'I thought you wanted to head back to shore? Isn't there a storm blowing in?'

'We're all right for a while.' He moved back towards the sun-chairs and picked up the bottle of wine to hold it out questioningly towards her.

'Well, I was on lemonade, but...' She shrugged. 'Why not...? I'll have a small glass.'

'Why not, indeed.'

She frowned as she heard that note in his voice again.

He poured the glass for her and handed it across. As their eyes met a shiver went through her.

She had been so anxious for David and Laura to go. Had longed to be alone with Pearce so that she could tell him everything. Now that the moment had arrived she was starting to think that maybe it wasn't a good idea to blurt out the truth. Perhaps she should choose her time more carefully. He didn't seem to be in a good frame of mind.

She remembered suddenly that they had been arguing before Laura arrived. 'You're not still angry with me...are you?' she asked him cautiously.

He put a hand to his cheek, as if reflecting on the way she had struck him. Then he grinned at her. 'I suppose I asked for it... No, I'm not angry about that.'

She started to relax. 'I'm sorry I've asked all those stupid questions about Jody. I—'

'They're not stupid questions,' he corrected her. 'I can understand why you want to know about her.'

'I don't think you can.' She ran an agitated hand through her hair. She didn't know where to begin with her confession. She was frightened...terribly frightened of his reaction.

He reached out and touched her face. 'I can't seem to

keep my hands off you,' he murmured. 'I've never felt like this before.'

She felt a tremor race through her. She opened her mouth to say something. She couldn't allow her emotions to take over. She needed to tell him who she was and get everything straight before she gave in to the weakness he stirred up so easily inside her.

He put a finger over her lips. 'And, before you ask. I have certainly never felt like this about Jody.' His lips curved in a wry smile.

'I wasn't going to ask.' She tried to move away from him, but his hand held her arm.

'I want to make love to you, Catherine. I want to make love to you now.'

The urgency in his voice and in his eyes made her whole body go into chaos.

'We need to talk first, Pearce...I...' Her voice trembled and halted as his lips met hers.

'We can talk later. I promise you that.'

He stood up from the chair and held his hand out to her.

Her eyes were shadowed with doubt...with temptation. She wanted him so much, but it felt so wrong. Leaving aside the fact that she had lied to him, there was still Jody...Poppy...to consider.

'Pearce, I don't want to be the cause of splitting up a family.' Her voice was unsteady. 'I really don't—'

'There isn't a family to split.'

Cathy frowned. 'No matter how you feel about marrying Jody, you still have Poppy and you are still a family.' Her voice trembled with emotion and with the weight of her guilt.

He shook his head. 'Poppy is not my daughter, Catherine.'

There it was, the answer to the question that everyone

wanted to know. She stared at him in stunned amazement. 'But I thought—'

'I know what you thought.' He cut across her heavily and then pulled her to her feet. 'But you were wrong.'

'So, who is Poppy's father?' Her voice was incredulous. 'Why is she here with you?'

'So many questions.' He stroked her hair back from her face in a tender caress that made her body tingle. 'But all I want to do is make love to you.'

'Pearce—'

She never got to finish what she was saying because he kissed her. His lips were druggingly persuasive, compelling, demanding.

She leaned against him and her arms sneaked up around his shoulders as she kissed him back with every ounce of feeling inside her.

'Later we can talk about everything.' He pulled away from her and she looked up at him with a deep, intense longing.

'I'll tell you about Jody and you can tell me your life story, if you want.' His voice dropped to a seductive whisper. 'But right now I can only think of one thing.'

CHAPTER TEN

THE cabin was dark after the brightness of the sun and it took a moment for Cathy's eyes to adjust.

It was stylish. The walls were wood panelled, in keeping with the floor and the doors. A curtain in bright Liberty fabric adorned the porthole and a matching duvet covered the large wooden bed.

Cathy's eyes lingered on that bed and a shiver of apprehension flooded through her.

Giving in to her desire was, in all probability, going to make matters worse. How could you make love to someone when you had lied to them—deceived them?

'Leave the door open in case Poppy wakes up.' Pearce's voice was brisk. He seemed almost businesslike for a moment as he put the two glasses of wine on the bedside table and then took off his shirt.

He sat down on the end of the bed and then looked over to where she still stood just inside the doorway. 'Having doubts?' His voice softened.

The return of gentle persuasion to his tone immediately made her feel a little better.

'Yes.' Her voice was heavy with uncertainty.

'Come here.' He held out a hand to her.

The coolly sensuous command made her senses reel.

She moved towards him slowly. When she stopped in front of him her waist was on a level with his eyes.

'Now, then.' He murmured the words almost to himself as leisurely and deliberately he started to unbutton the front of her shorts.

She stood quite still, allowing him to undress her. Her shorts were thrown carelessly across the floor. She was only wearing a scanty pair of pants beneath them but he made no attempt to take them off her. Instead he ran a finger playfully around the lacy string, then he bent his head and kissed the satin material that covered the soft core of her femininity.

She caught her breath on a shudder of exquisite ecstasy and her eyes closed against the searing heat of the moment.

'Do you want me?'

It took a while for her brain to even formulate the question, let alone the answer. She was eaten away with a yearning that had completely taken over every thought, every inch of her body.

'You know I do.' Her hands moved to the silky softness of his hair as she instinctively moved her body closer.

'Then show me.' He moved away from her and sat back against the bedhead.

Her heart thumped unsteadily in her chest and she looked at him, her eyes wide and questioning.

'Take off your top.'

There was a momentary quiver of shyness inside her, but it was quelled by a much more forceful, urgent need for him.

Slowly she obeyed him and stripped the soft jersey T-shirt off to throw it beside her shorts. Her breasts were naked and heavy. She could feel his eyes moving over them almost as if he was touching them.

'Now the panties.'

Impatient for him now, she pulled the flimsy panties off. When she looked back at him his eyes had moved past her and she realised that he was looking at her reflection in the mirror behind her.

'You have a beautiful body.' His eyes moved back to her. 'The body of a siren.'

She smiled. 'May I come to bed?' The words were

whispered playfully, in deference to the game of male domination that she had been following.

'Please may I come to bed,' he corrected her, his voice firm, his eyes unsmiling.

'Pearce, I...' She was confused for a moment, worried by his mood.

His eyes moved over her naked body, taking in the way her long blonde hair almost reached her up-tilted breasts. 'You can't blame me for wanting to make sure.' He moved towards her then. 'For all I know, you might change your mind the way you did last night.'

'I won't change my mind.' She closed her eyes as his fingers ran teasingly over her breasts. Then she caught her breath sharply as his lips covered one nipple, his mouth warm against the coolness of her skin.

'So say it then.' The order was implicit as he pulled back from her.

She clenched her hands in a kind of helplessness. She wanted him so much that it was like some kind of sweet torment. 'You know I want you, Pearce.'

He smiled then, a triumphant, attractive smile. Then he stood up and removed the rest of his clothing.

Her chest felt tight with longing, her breasts hard with the need to feel his hands—his lips—against them again. When he caught her around the waist and swung her off her feet it took her by surprise.

His strength astounded her. Her breath left her body with a gasp as he put her down on the bed with no attempt at gentleness.

Her hair was a wild tangle against the covers, her eyes wide and filled with a mixture of hunger and apprehension as they met his.

There were a brief few moments when they just stared at each other.

Cathy's breath was coming in short, sharp waves. She was aware of everything about him—from the hard,

muscled length of his body pressing down against hers
to the roughness of the hairs on his chest prickling
against her sensitive breast.

She felt him parting her legs with his knee. Then suddenly he was inside her.

The shock was intense. She had expected him to kiss
her some more...she had expected it to be leisurely. But
magically as he started to move rhythmically she was
consumed by a pleasure so deep that the world seem to
spin on it.

She could only think of Pearce and how much she
wanted him, all of him—body, soul, mind. She savoured
the feeling of having him close inside, wanted the blissful wonder of it to go on for ever.

He kissed her eyelids, her ears, whispering against her
skin how he'd like to make love to her again and again—
make her truly his.

The words kindled her passion, making her rise higher
and higher on the pleasure scale until she could only
cling precariously to the last thread of control.

Then she peaked in wave after wave of ecstasy, crying
his name and raking her hands down his back as she felt
him tense and join her in the spiral of wild sweet won-
derment.

For a long moment they just lay there in each other's
arms. Cathy had never felt so tired, her body drained of
all energy. It also felt warmly relaxed, perfectly sated.

'You are so beautiful.' He whispered the words as he
eased himself from her and she reached up to hold him.
She didn't want him to leave her. She never wanted him
to leave her.

'Darling Pearce,' she murmured dreamily then, curled
in his arms, she drifted into a deep sleep.

There was something different about the bed...some-
thing strange. Cathy stretched, feeling disoriented.

She opened her eyes and looked at the unfamiliar wooden ceiling. The room seemed to move suddenly.

She sat up as memory returned and with it a sudden feeling of anxiety.

She was alone in the bedroom.

'Pearce?' Her voice was a tremulous sound in the silence as she wondered if he was in the adjoining bathroom. There was no reply.

Quickly she got up. Her clothes were scattered around the floor. The memory of the way she had undressed for him—the way she had given herself to him—was piercingly vital. It made her feel alive with so many mixed emotions that she had to sit down again on the bed.

It was too late for recriminations. She had given in to weakness and allowed her emotions full reign. The fact that she had done so before telling Pearce the truth had been a grim mistake. She was sure of that. Even so, the passion that had been between them had been so intense, so real that she felt her spirits lift. Surely they would work things out. Pearce had to feel the same way about her.

The room seemed to tilt and for a breathless moment she wondered if she was light-headed. Then she realised that the boat was moving. She frowned and went over to the porthole. She could see the coast in the distance and they were moving at speed.

Quickly, she dressed and went out into the corridor and through the galley. She glanced at Poppy's carrycot on the way past but the child wasn't in it.

It was cooler up on deck now. A salty breeze whipped against her face in a refreshing way.

The boat was skipping over the waves as she sailed parallel with the coast. The white sails were fully up now and they made a flapping, ruffling noise as the wind skimmed them.

She found Pearce on the bridge, Poppy safely strapped into her carry chair beside him.

'Well, good evening.' He looked around as he heard her soft plimsolls on the wood of the deck.

'Good evening, captain.' She tried to match his brisk tone, but her eyes veered away as they met his.

'We should be home in a few minutes.' He turned his attention back to the wheel of the ship.

She watched him silently. He had changed into jeans and a navy blue sweatshirt and he looked casually relaxed.

Cathy longed for him to reach out a hand and pull her against him. She wanted to snuggle into the curve of his arm and tell him how much she loved him, but she didn't dare. There was something about his tone of voice...and the way his attention was so firmly on what he was doing...that forbade such an intimacy.

'Have I been asleep for very long?' she asked instead, taking the adjacent seat to him and picking Poppy up from her chair.

'Hours. I didn't like to disturb you.' He flicked her a glance that was at one and the same time cool yet amused. 'Thought you were probably tired out.'

'Yes.' She didn't know what else to say. She felt lost suddenly.

The sun was starting to go down. It lit the sky in a vivid flamingo pink then faded to a dusky rose, reflecting on the water and on the coast line—making the world look surreal.

She held Poppy close against her. The warmth of the baby was reassuring. It wasn't that she was cold but shivers were racing through her body.

She saw the jetty at the bottom of Pearce's estate and for no real reason regret welled up inside her.

'You know we need to talk, Pearce,' she said quietly as he pressed the buttons to lower the sails.

'I haven't forgotten.' He slanted a very cool look at her.

Cathy frowned. There was something wrong. She wanted to catch hold of him and demand to know what it was. Had she not pleased him in bed...? The thought was almost ridiculous as she remembered the excessive pleasure of the afternoon.

It seemed much more likely that now he had enjoyed the intimacy of her body he had lost interest in her. The notion sent a pang of such acute anguish through her that she fell silent.

She watched as he negotiated the difficulties of bringing the ship smoothly alongside the jetty.

Henri came hurrying down the path and then waited patiently as Pearce threw the ropes for him to tie up and secure the vessel.

It was pitch dark as they disembarked.

'You deal with Poppy.' Pearce's voice was curt. 'I have a few things to do down here before I can come up to the house.'

Poppy was tearful as Cathy carried her up the steep path towards the lights of the villa.

Cathy couldn't help but sympathise with her. She felt tearful herself.

She went in through the back door and there was a sudden glorious feeling of having come home. The kitchen was warm and there was a delicious smell of cinnamon and baking.

She put Poppy in her high chair and then opened the oven to investigate.

A casserole bubbled invitingly on the lower shelf and on the top there was an apple pie. She closed the door with a frown. Either Henri had hidden talents as a cook or maybe he had raided the deep freeze.

There wasn't time to ponder the question. Poppy was grouchy. She wanted feeding and changing. Lifting the child up, she decided to deal with her in the nursery…perhaps give her a bath and then try and settle her down for the evening.

It was a full two hours before Cathy put the child down in her cot and there had been no sound of Pearce's presence in the house.

She sat down on the settee in the nursery and leaned her head wearily back against it. She felt exhausted, both emotionally and physically.

Footsteps sounded in the corridor and Cathy looked up as Pearce stopped outside the door. 'How's Poppy?'

He sounded tired, she thought. Almost as tired as she felt.

'She's asleep. Went off without a murmur. Must have been all that fresh air.'

'Good.' He turned and opened his bedroom door.

'Pearce?'

He looked back at her calmly. 'Yes?'

'Is…is there anything wrong?'

A shadow of a smile crossed the handsome features. 'What could be wrong?'

'Well…I…' She shook her head and stood up. She needed to clear the atmosphere. It struck her that she could be imagining his coolness. She was weighed down by the guilt of her deception and it was playing on her mind, colouring everything. 'I think we should talk,' she said quietly.

'Yes, we should.' He opened his bedroom door. 'But not now, Catherine. I'm tired.'

She didn't get a chance to say anything else because he went into his room and closed the door firmly behind him.

Cathy stared at the door. She felt hurt, insulted. To be so coldly rebuffed after the passion they had shared was humiliating, to say the least.

She didn't know how long she stood there. Then anger surfaced through the pain and she went across to his door and, without even bothering to knock, she walked in.

He was standing with his back to her and he was talking to someone on the phone. 'I've probably said too much,' he was saying irately.

He didn't appear to have heard her entering the room because he didn't turn. Cathy was about to say something, make her presence known, when he said impatiently, 'Well, she knows that I'm not Poppy's father, but she doesn't know that you are my half-sister or that Jonathan Briars is Poppy's father—'

Cathy moved in surprise at that statement and he whirled around.

There was a moment's silence. Pearce's eyes narrowed on her, then he said briskly, 'Look, Jody, I'll have to ring you back.'

Cathy watched as he put the phone back down on the bedside table. 'Poppy is your niece?' Her voice was small and uncertain as slowly the pieces started to fit together.

'That's really none of your business.'

She flinched at the cold tone and took a couple of steps further into the room.

'I really wouldn't come in here right now, if I were you, Catherine.' There was a steely warning in his voice, in his eyes.

She closed the door behind her. 'Why not?' She looked at him, her head held high. 'Pearce, why are you behaving like this? I think you owe me a little more than just a cold brush-off, don't you?'

'Oh, you think I owe you something, do you?' His voice was heavy with sarcasm.

She frowned. She had been prepared for indifference, but not this jeering kind of contempt.

'Pearce...I...' She shook her head helplessly.

'Don't look at me like that.' His voice was flat.

'Like what?' Her eyes shimmered. 'Like someone who has been hurt? Like someone who feels used? Well, I'm sorry, but that is how you are starting to make me feel.'

'Am I?' Calmly he turned away from her and unbuttoned his shirt. 'If you wouldn't mind leaving, I'm going to have a shower.'

'Why are you shutting me out?' Her voice was low and trembling. 'This afternoon...this afternoon you were so—'

'Passionate?' He supplied the word for her, his lips twisting drily. 'I'm not shutting you out, Catherine, but be warned that if you stay in here then I will want to make love to you again.'

Her cheeks burned with colour. 'I didn't mean shutting me out like that.'

'Didn't you?'

'You know I didn't.' Her eyes were bright with emotion. 'I don't understand you, Pearce.'

'I don't understand myself much at this moment.' He threw his shirt on the chair. 'All I know is that I had you this afternoon and now, despite the fact that you make me blazingly mad, I want you again.'

The heat that filled her body at those words was incredible. She felt as if she had stepped into the Tropics. 'Why are you so angry?' Her voice trembled.

He slanted a hard brooding look at her. 'The thing is, Catherine Fielding, that I don't want to feel this desire for you.'

She stared at him, hurt beyond words. 'Are you in love with someone else?' It was a low whisper of anguish.

'I wondered when you'd get around to asking me some more questions.' His laughter was mirthless.

'You're good, you know, really good. You almost have me believing that lost, vulnerable little-girl look.'

'I don't know what you mean.' Her heart thudded unsteadily.

'Really?' One eyebrow lifted quizzically. 'Tell you what, why don't you join me in the shower? Then I'll explain everything to you...tell you how I found out that Jody Sterling was my sister.' His voice was heavy with sarcasm. 'Or perhaps your little recorder won't work in there? And another problem. Even if we leave the window wide open your boyfriend probably won't be able to get any...decent...photographs.'

She felt as if she were back on board the boat as the floor seemed to tilt under her feet. 'You know about me.'

'Of course I bloody know.' He started to unbutton his Levis. So, what do you say, do you fancy joining me in the shower? Or are the drawbacks a bit too much for you?'

Her eyes veered away from him. 'You don't understand—'

'Don't I?' His voice was scathing. 'I think I understand all too well. Now let's see... You are supposed to play the vamp, get all the information you can and David was supposed to be taking the photographs.'

'You heard David talking to me today?' Cathy asked, her face stiff.

'The end of the conversation, yes. But I knew about you before that.'

'How long?' His matter-of-factness was more chilling than if he had shouted at her. 'How long have you known?'

'About ten minutes after you first walked through my front door.'

He walked to the bedside table and, opening it, he threw a file on the bed beside her. Pages fluttered to the floor.

Numbly she bent to pick up a few of them. She blinked in surprise as she saw what it was.

All her personal history was in that file. Which schools she had attended. Her address, a list of all the jobs she had held down and for how long. There was even a copy of a character reference that one of her old bosses had given her.

She stooped to pick up the rest of the papers. There was a whole stack of articles she had written over the past six months. On the top of the pile was the article she had written on modern-day child care.

'You've certainly done your homework.' She straightened and looked at him accusingly.

'Of course I did.' He was unperturbed. 'I'd hardly just let anyone look after Poppy. I needed to make sure you were at least stable and capable.'

'How did you get this information?' Her eyes narrowed on him.

'I paid for it.' He smiled calmly. 'You can get almost anything if the price is right. It was faxed and on my desk within an hour of your arrival.'

'Some seedy private eye, I take it?'

'I thought he was pretty efficient myself. But you did give me your real name, which was fairly helpful.'

'But why?' Her voice trembled almost uncontrollably as she looked at the papers in her hand. 'Why didn't you just throw me out immediately...or say something?'

'I've asked myself the same question. I guess I couldn't resist.'

She looked back at him, her heart turning somersaults as hope filtered through.

'My first impulse was to throw you out. Then you came down to my study, looking seductively gorgeous, and I was intrigued.' He shrugged. 'I'm a red-blooded male and I have to admit that once the deception had started I wanted to know where it would lead. How far you would go. And you went all the way...didn't you, Catherine?'

Humiliation scalded her. She was on the verge of tears but she wouldn't let them fall—that would be the final indignity. 'I can't believe how calculating you've been.' Her voice was a mere whisper.

'How like a woman to turn the situation around.' He shook his head, a mocking expression on his handsome features. 'You lie to me, you deceive me, try every trick in the book to find out about my private affairs. Then you accuse me of being calculating.'

He started to take his jeans off. 'I'm going to have my shower now.' He slanted a provocative look at her. 'I take it you are not joining me?'

'Get lost.' Her voice was frozen with absolute fury.

His mocking laughter followed her from the room. 'If you play with fire, Catherine, you should expect to be burnt.'

CHAPTER ELEVEN

CATHY flung her belongings into her suitcase. Her one thought was to get away from here. She didn't care where to. Anywhere would do, anywhere she could bury her head and die of shame.

She could hardly fasten her case her hands were trembling so much. Finally she clicked the locks into position and then turned to get the keys of her hire car out of her handbag. She couldn't find them, and in frustration she turned the bag upside down and tipped the contents out on the covers of her bed. There were no keys.

She cursed under her breath and tried to remember where she had put them. Frantically, she opened the drawers next to her bed, then in desperation she started to look on the floor. But they weren't anywhere.

She sat down on the bed and her body shook with panic.

She couldn't understand it. She was almost sure that she had put the keys into her handbag. All right, the car hadn't been used since she had arrived, but it wasn't that long ago! She cringed as she remembered just how short a time it was. So much had happened...so much.

How could she have fallen in love so quickly...? How could she have let the emotion inside her heart take her over? She berated herself again and again. Then she leaned her head into her hands as helpless tears blurred her vision.

The worst thing of all was that Pearce believed that she had deliberately set out to seduce him, just to get information.

She could hardly blame Pearce for thinking what he

did…for saying what he had said. The evidence was pretty damning.

But she hadn't set out to seduce him. Her skin burned at the thought. She wasn't a *femme fatale*…it wasn't in her nature. She was an ordinary woman—one who had fallen in love with the wrong man. It had happened to millions of other women. She wasn't evil, she wasn't unusual. Well, the circumstances had been unusual. But she had only been trying to do her job.

Pearce had known about her deception from the start. He had gone along with it. Then he had cold-bloodedly taken advantage of the situation.

Her body shuddered at the memory of this afternoon.

What was it he had said? 'If you play with fire you should expect to be burnt.'

Her head jerked up and she blinked away her tears as anger came to her rescue. She wasn't going to feel sorry for herself. She had made a mistake…followed her heart instead of her head. Pearce Tyrone should also expect to be burned. Her lips curved a little at the thought. 'Preferably in hell,' she muttered to herself under her breath.

She stood up and swept the contents of her bag together then, picking up her suitcase, she left the room.

Before leaving the nursery, she checked on Poppy. The child was sleeping peacefully. Cathy's heart constricted painfully as her eyes moved over the tousled blonde curls that framed the little face. There was a delicate tinge of colour on the baby's plump cheeks, her lips were parted in a soft O and she had one little thumb poised as if she had been sucking on it. Cathy leaned over and kissed one cheek gently, breathing in the baby-sweet smell of talcum powder and fresh linen.

Then she straightened quickly as tears threatened to fall. She was going to miss Poppy.

She picked up her suitcase and hurried down the stairs.

She was in the process of searching the kitchen for her car keys when Pearce came in. Her whole body stiffened with anger, with awareness, as she flicked a glance over at him.

He had changed into a fawn pair of trousers and a cream-coloured shirt. He looked at her with a raised eyebrow. 'Looking for something?' he asked coolly.

She made no reply. She didn't think she was capable of speaking to him without shouting. Furiously she continued with her search, opening drawers and looking on the hooks behind the back door.

'Perhaps I can help?'

Something about his tone made her glance back at him.

He was leaning against the kitchen counter and in his hand he was nonchalantly dangling her car keys.

'Where did you get those?' she demanded breathlessly.

'Same place I got this from.' Calmly he held up a roll of film.

'You've been going through my handbag.' Her voice was shrill with fury.

'Not very pleasant to have your privacy invaded, is it, Catherine?' he asked softly.

He smiled as he noticed the furious flare of colour in her cheeks.

'You are a first-class rat, Tyrone,' she muttered darkly.

'Coming from someone who has deceived me, who has used every feminine wile to get close to me for her own devious reasons, I'll take that as a compliment.'

His equanimity made her feel like throwing something at him. She longed to break that cool façade of his and really hurt him. Her hands clenched and unclenched in futile fists at her side.

'I know what I did was wrong, Pearce, but what you did was despicable.' Her voice shook and for a moment she was frightened that her anger would crack and that he would see the vulnerable hurt person inside.

'The only thing I did was play you at your own game. You did the rest yourself.'

She moved swiftly for him. 'Give me my keys.' She reached to take them but he was too quick for her and swung them out of reach.

'Patience, Catherine,' he said softly.

'I demand that you give me my keys.' Her heart was thumping furiously against her breast.

'You are in no position to demand anything.' He smiled, then pocketed both the keys and the roll of film. 'First we have some talking to do.'

'I've done all the talking I want to do with you,' she told him positively.

'Yes...I suppose you have.' He murmured the words almost thoughtfully. 'You've got all the answers now, haven't you, Catherine...? No need to flutter your eyelashes anymore.'

She took a deep breath. 'I have never fluttered my eyelashes at you.'

He merely laughed at that.

Cathy watched as he calmly made his way over to the oven and started to take out the food inside. 'I don't know about you, but I'm hungry.'

'If you think that I am going to eat with you—'

'You've suddenly become very choosy.' He took the lid off the casserole and looked inside. 'A little over-done, but it should be all right.'

'Who cooked that, anyway?' she asked him in a brittle voice.

'Henri. He's really a very good chef.'

'Then why did you need a cook?'

'I didn't. I just thought that the busier I could keep you the less mischief you could get up to.'

She remembered the way she had tried to cook dinner

last night...how she had scrubbed at the burnt
pans...and a wave of renewed fury hit her. 'I hate you,
Pearce Tyrone.'

'Don't act like the aggrieved party, Catherine,' he said
firmly. 'I know damn well that you sent for a take-away
yesterday. I have the whole pitiful episode on tape.'

This took her aback for a moment. Her eyes narrowed.
'What do you mean, you've got it on tape?'

'The security cameras on the gates filmed the van
from Le Gardin, arriving at eight-thirty. Then you left
the gates open for your boyfriend, who arrived at eight
forty-five precisely.'

'So you knew about David even before his appearance
on your boat today?'

'Oh, yes. I think that was what made me really mad.'

'I don't follow you.'

He put the lid back on the dish and then turned to
look at her. 'The whole thing struck me as comical until
I realised that you weren't in it alone. I think up until
then I would have given you your interview. I most certainly would have given it to you if you had asked up
front right from the beginning.'

'No, you wouldn't.' Her voice was positive. 'You're
just trying to make me feel worse.'

'And am I succeeding?'

'Yes.' She glared at him, furious fires of regret and
anger burning her up. 'Whatever you might think, I
didn't set out to seduce you...and I wasn't working with
David Collins. The gates were a mistake.'

Why she started to explain herself was beyond
her...she hated him, she really did.

She could tell from the expression on his face that he
didn't believe her and his next words confirmed it. 'It's
incredible how innocent and virtuous you sound. I'm
almost tempted to believe you, even though I know the
truth.'

He moved closer to her. 'You're a good actress, Catherine. In fact, more than a few times I've been seriously drawn towards believing in the caring, virtuous person you have been playing. I've been starting to wonder about my own sanity.'

'Well, don't wonder any more,' she told him. 'I'll personally vouch for you being certifiable.'

'Thanks.'

Her heart thudded erratically as she realised suddenly that her anger was dropping, that the atmosphere between them was changing. She swallowed hard. 'About this afternoon... Did you really cold-bloodedly mean for...it to happen?' She shook her head helplessly. She felt so bad about it...so used. 'It wasn't...fair of you, Pearce... It really wasn't right.'

'And what you've been doing is right?' One eyebrow lifted, mocking her.

'I think you've got ice-water running in your veins.'

'I think you've got double standards.' He reached out a hand to touch her face and she flinched away. 'It's all right for you to try and seduce me, but not vice versa.'

'I didn't say that. And, anyway, I wasn't.' She was confused by his closeness...it sent a wash of panic through her.

'Pull the other one, Catherine. You've led me right to the brink—flirting with me, wandering around naked, telling me openly you wanted me. Then, right at the last moment, you'd say, but what about Jody?'

'I asked about Jody because I was...concerned.'

'Concerned about getting a good story.' He shook his head and trailed a finger down the side of her face. The caress was erotic and at the same time it was dangerous. It reminded her of this afternoon and the pleasure of being in his arms. 'Don't come over all moral on me, Cathy. You wanted your story and you were prepared to go to any lengths.'

'Stop it, Pearce.' She tried to move away from him, but found that she was back up against the kitchen counter.

'I've enjoyed the game, Catherine—'

'Well, I haven't.' She cut across him heatedly.

One eyebrow lifted and the mocking look returned to his eyes. 'You mean you didn't enjoy this afternoon?'

The silky voice, the gleam in his eye, made her temperature flare. It was unbearable that he should laugh at her like this. She had her pride.

'Oh, you like to flatter yourself, don't you?' Her voice was bitter with contempt. 'Well, let me tell you that I didn't feel anything for you this afternoon.' Her eyes slid away from his as his features darkened. She wanted so much to hurt him, to hit out. If the only way she could do that was to strike his male ego then so be it. He already believed the worst of her—she might as well turn it to her advantage. 'I was playing the vamp…remember?'

'And you did it so well.' His voice was low. No anger, but a hint of something…something much more powerful than anger.

Then he lowered his head towards hers. She tried to twist her face away from him but he captured her lips with ease. She fought against the seductive pressure of his kiss, tried to push him away. She put her free hand on his shoulder to shove him as hard as she could but he murmured something huskily against her skin. The sound of his voice, the feel of his body so close made her respond to him suddenly. It was almost instinctive, as if her body remembered the glories of the afternoon and traitorously cried out for them against everything her mind tried to say.

Her lips yielded passionately to his. The kiss could only have lasted for a few seconds and then he released her.

'If that was acting then you deserve an Oscar.'

She was somewhat mollified by the fact that his voice wasn't steady. There was a hunger in his eyes for just a moment as he looked at her.

She raked a trembling hand through the long length of her blonde hair, appalled by the way she had just responded to him. 'Don't you ever touch me again.'

He smiled. 'Such outrage in your voice, such a contradiction from your lips.'

She squirmed inwardly. He was right. No matter what he said or did, she couldn't deny the way she felt about him. The knowledge made her feel helpless.

He turned away from her and stood for a moment with his back to her.

She took a deep breath, trying to steady herself—trying to think in a rational manner.

'So, what do you intend to write in your newspaper about Jody Sterling?' He spun to look at her again, his eyes narrowed and watchful.

'Ah!' For just a moment a gleam of satisfaction showed in her eyes. From feeling totally helpless—totally at his mercy—there was suddenly a chink in his armour and she realised that she did have some power. She could hurt him, make him worried.

'I don't exactly know what I shall write about Jody Sterling.' she said with a shrug, 'but I know exactly what I'm going to write about you. I'm going to tell everyone that you are the coldest man I have ever met... I'm going to tell the whole damn world how you deliberately used me.'

'So, in other words, you intend to write a completely one-sided, trashy article.' He shook his head. 'I don't know why that should surprise me about you...but it does. Is the truth not going to be a factor in your little composition at all?'

'That is the truth.' She forced herself to look directly into his eyes.

'I think, if we are going to be pedantically precise, the truth is that you were prepared to sell your body for a story.' His voice dripped with sarcasm. 'And I don't know about my being the coldest man you have ever met because, despite what you say, you respond to me totally.'

She caught her breath. 'You really are beneath contempt.' Her voice came out in a shaky rush.

'Because I remind you of the truth of the situation?' He raised a dark eyebrow.

Furiously she lifted her hand but he caught hold of it before she could make contact with his face.

'I've let you strike me once today.' His voice was low and controlled. 'But now I'm calling the tune, and you are the one who is dancing.'

'That's what you think.' She twisted away from him. 'I'm the one holding all the cards. I know the truth about Jody... I know that Poppy's father is a prominent politician.'

'And you'd really stoop so low as to print that story— even though you don't know the true facts?' His voice was hard with contempt.

'A secret like that can't be kept for ever. Someone will let it out.' She tried to sound nonchalant. But deep down she knew that she was bluffing, knew that she was just trying to break through that cool exterior of his...the way he was so easily able to break her. She wasn't going to write anything about Jody Sterling.

'I don't think it would come out. No one, except for Laura, knows the truth.'

'Laura?' Cathy felt suddenly as if he had hit her.

'Yes.' He shrugged. 'But she is perfectly trustworthy.'

Unlike her, Cathy thought with more than a tinge of bitterness. Suddenly she realised that she wasn't holding any cards, any sway, over Pearce Tyrone. She cared too much to write anything about him. He was the one able to manipulate every string on her heart.

That he had confided in Laura hurt unbelievably.

'Look, Catherine, write what you want about me, but don't write about Jody. The truth could hurt too many people.'

'All right.' Her voice was low. All the anger had gone out of her. 'Can I have my car keys now?' She held out her hand.

He looked at her suspiciously. Then slowly he took her keys and held them out to her.

'Thanks.' She snatched them from him and briskly moved past him out into the hallway to pick up her suitcase.

'Where will you go? The air strike is still on, you know.'

She looked around at him. 'I'll go to a hotel.'

'Where, no doubt, David Collins will be waiting.' His voice took on an abrasive quality. 'I suppose you will waste no time wrapping your arms around him and telling him all the juicy details you learnt about Poppy's parentage?'

'You seem very sure that Laura won't already have told him.' Cathy's voice shook slightly. It hurt...really hurt to know that he didn't believe her when she had said that she wouldn't use the information, that he thought more of Laura than he did about her.

'Are you going back to Collins now?'

'Probably.' She flashed him a defiant look. If he wanted to believe the worst of her then he could. She hoped he would lie awake at night, worrying about what she might write—at least it would make up in some small way for the fact that she would lie awake, longing for him.

'What was it you said, Pearce, "If you play with fire then you should expect to be burnt"?' Then calmly she walked away.

CHAPTER TWELVE

'GET in here, Fielding.' Mike's voice boomed across the busy newsroom and a number of Cathy's colleagues sent her sympathetic looks as she got up hurriedly from her desk.

Cathy wasn't surprised by her editor's tone of voice. Ever since she had got back from the South of France six weeks ago he had been finding fault in everything she did.

She knew very well that it was because she had failed to write any kind of article on Pearce Tyrone. She was probably lucky that he hadn't fired her. As it was, he was now making her life as unpleasant as possible by giving her the most awful assignments, things that a raw journalist would be expected to do. It was a deliberate snub and it was testing her patience to the limit.

Taking a deep breath, she went into his office and closed the glass door on the rest of the newsroom. It was bad enough that she should have to endure further insults, without the whole of the office hearing.

Mike sat behind his desk, a big bulldog of a man with heavy jowls and narrow slanting eyes. He glared at her.

'This piece on the new Edwin factory.' He stabbed a finger accusingly at the copy in front of him.

'Yes?' Cathy waited patiently. She knew that there was nothing wrong with that piece. She had spent ages checking her facts, she had got plenty of information across and it was interesting and to the point. It had taken her ages, far longer than she would normally have spent on such a mundane assignment.

'It's not punchy enough.'

'Punchy?' Cathy stared at her boss and felt a sudden urge to make something very punchy, preferably across his thick jaw.

'There is not enough meat in it.'

'Well, I know that,' Cathy said patiently. 'I told you that before you sent me out there. It's not a particularly juicy story. I can't do much about that unless you want me to dream up something, fabricate a few facts.'

'And you couldn't do that, could you, Cathy?' His voice was almost a snarl. 'Just like you couldn't write anything about Pearce Tyrone. What was it you said...nothing to report? Not ethical to write anything because you couldn't be sure of any facts?'

'Well, you don't want us to be sued, do you?'

He shook his head, but more in anger than anything else. 'Even David Collins didn't come up with a decent photograph. Except that one of you and Tyrone kissing in his car and I think every newspaper managed to get that.'

Nausea started to curl in Cathy's stomach. She tried to fight the feeling and face up to Mike squarely. 'I've explained about that.'

'In a fashion.' He leaned back in his chair and sighed. 'Oh, I know the man is a charmer, a womaniser. I've only got to look at the photographs that came in yesterday.'

'What photographs?'

He leaned towards a tray on the counter next to him and took out two glossy photographs, both of Tyrone leaving a restaurant—his arm snugly around Laura Houston's shoulders. The woman was looking adoringly up at him, a smile curving her lips.

'She is his agent. It was probably a business dinner.' Even as she spoke the words she was aware of a wedge of pain hitting her hard.

'We don't know what is going on, do we? Because you didn't find anything out.'

'How long are you going to spend punishing me for that, Mike? Because, I'm warning you, I'm not going to stand for much more.' Her voice rose as her temper started to crack. She wasn't sure if her anger was generated by the mere sight of Pearce Tyrone with his arm around Laura, or her boss's attitude. She did know, however, that she should watch her words. She couldn't afford to lose her job, not now that she needed it more than ever.

It was a relief when the phone rang, deflating the situation and taking Mike's attention from her.

He snatched up the receiver and barked into it.

The nausea grew worse, kicking into her with vicious intensity. Cathy struggled to contain it for a few seconds more, then she had to hurry from the room towards the ladies' toilets.

She was in there for fifteen minutes and when she came out she felt weak. She splashed her face with cold water, rinsed her mouth and then studied her reflection in the mirror. She looked pale, washed out. She was losing weight, something that surprised her. She had thought that when you were pregnant you gained weight. Her mouth twisted in a painful way. But then she was only six weeks...six weeks since she had lain in Pearce's arms. It felt like an eternity ago.

'You OK, Cathy?' One of the other girls from her office came in and looked at her with some concern.

'Yes...fine.' She opened her handbag and searched for a lipstick.

'You shouldn't let Mike get to you,' the girl said angrily. 'He's been really horrible with you lately. You should tell him—'

'It's all right, Sally.' Cathy put her lipstick on and then snapped her bag closed. 'But thank you for your

concern.' Then she left before the girl could offer her
any more advice.

She'd had advice on how to handle Mike from practically everyone in the office. They were all worried about
her. Cathy didn't think she could cope with either their
concern or Mike's anger. She felt as if she was hanging
on to her control by the merest thread.

When she got back to her editor's office she expected
him to shout at her again. But he stared at her for a
moment and then miraculously he smiled.

'Got another assignment for you,' he said.

'Yes?' Cathy looked at him suspiciously.

'Get yourself down to that French restaurant on the
wharf.'

Cathy knew which restaurant he was talking about. It
was virtually next door to the newspaper.

'Now?' Cathy's stomach protested violently at the
mere thought of being in the same room as food.

'Yes, now.' He glared at her with a return of some of
his former aggression.

'Mike, I don't feel very well.' She dropped her voice
to a gentle persuasive tone. 'Could you get someone else
to cover whatever it is? I think I'll have to go home and
lie down.'

'No, I can't use anyone else, it has to be you.' He
started to raise his voice and then, as if thinking better
of losing his temper, he said in a quieter voice, 'Order
yourself a good meal while you are in there. It will make
you feel better. They do superb garlic -mushrooms.'

'I can't, Mike,' Cathy said briskly. 'I'm sorry, I have
to go home.' She started to back out towards the door.
'I'll do it tomorrow afternoon...or send someone else.
I'll phone in and speak to you later.'

'Cathy, this is important. Your job could be—'

She closed the door on the rest of Mike's sentence.
She didn't want to hear any more of his threats. There

was just no way that she could face a restaurant at this moment, whether her job depended on it or not.

Quickly she gathered up her jacket from the back of her chair, switched off her computer terminal and headed for the lifts.

The newspaper was situated on the quayside. It was an area that at one time had been deserted and derelict. Now the old red brick warehouses had been restored and rejuvenated into modern offices. There were a few smart coffee-houses and restaurants, and the cobbled walkway beside the water was now a place where people enjoyed a stroll on a warm summer's day.

Today, however, it was virtually deserted. Despite the fact that it was the end of July, it was bitterly cold. The sky was a heavily laden slate grey, the wind that cut across the water reminiscent of a November day.

Cathy had moved here seven years ago and had been pleased to be away from the rush of the city centre. She had taken a steep mortgage on a little apartment just a few minutes' walk from the office. It had been an expensive move and she had bought it at a time when property prices were high, but she hadn't regretted it. Not until now.

As a single mother, she would never be able to afford her apartment. Even if she kept her job, child care was expensive.

She stopped walking and stared across the water. She tried to keep her mind occupied with the realities of having this baby, tried to think about money and how she would manage and therefore not dwell on Pearce. She didn't want to think about Pearce at all.

The photographs on Mike's desk blazed across her mind as soon as there was a gap in her businesslike thoughts. Pearce and Laura, laughing together, their arms around each other. She had asked Pearce so many questions about Jody...but all along it should have been Laura that she should have asked about.

There was a small boat with white sails, skimming backwards and forwards over the grey water. She could hear the distant fluttering sound of the wind in the sails. Despite the coldness of the day, the sound and the sight of those sails took her back to the South of France and the day she had spent on Pearce's yacht. She remembered Poppy's sweet smile, the sparkle of sunlight on water, the heat of passion, and how it had felt to be held and loved for just a brief interlude. Her eyes closed. She wouldn't cry.

'Catherine?'

For a moment she thought she had imagined the deep familiar voice. She wanted to see Pearce so badly that she almost imagined that she had conjured him up from her very soul.

She turned and rubbed a hand across her eyes, clearing the mist of tears.

He was standing beside her. A tall, handsome man, so familiar and dear to her yet a stranger in so many other ways. The shock was so intense that for a chaotic few seconds she didn't think she would be able to speak to him without breaking down.

His eyes swept over her appearance, and he frowned. She knew he was noticing how pale she was, how thin. She wondered if he was comparing her to Laura... beautiful, trustworthy Laura.

The thought made her eyes flash with sudden defiance. 'I thought that you were in the South of France.' Her voice was remarkably cool and she was proud of it.

'Got back yesterday.' His voice was gentle. 'Didn't you get my message?'

'What message?' She stared at him apprehensively.

'I rang your editor a little while ago—asked if we could meet for lunch.'

'The French restaurant?' she asked.

'That's right.' He nodded. 'I wanted to see you right away and I thought the quickest method was—'

'Are you trying to get me fired?' Her eyes blazed into his now.

He seemed taken aback by her anger. 'Of course not...'

'Well, you are going the right way about it.' She took a deep breath, trying to keep her voice below the shrill, accusing tone that she so desperately wanted to use. 'Have you any idea what kind of criticism and hostility I've had to put up with from my editor because I wouldn't write any kind of article about you?'

'I've been wondering what's happened. I keep watching your paper every day, waiting for you to put some kind of column together—'

'I said I wouldn't, and I haven't.' She glared at him with fury. 'And now you go and ring Mike and start it all over again.' She shook her head. 'What the hell were you thinking about?'

'You.'

The quiet answer only made her more furious. 'How you could destroy me completely? Get my boss to sack me? All right, Pearce, I know that I did the wrong thing by deceiving you the way I did... I know I shouldn't have stayed in your house under false pretences... But I did and I said I was sorry. Now why don't you leave me alone and stop trying to ruin my life?' She made to swing away from him but he grabbed her arm.

'Don't be so damn dramatic.' His voice was also angry. 'I'm not trying to ruin your life.'

'So, why ring my editor?'

He let go of her then. 'I told him we had some loose ends to tie up. That I had promised you an exclusive interview when I came back to London. I guess it was a clumsy way of trying to make amends to you.' He shrugged. 'I'm sorry, Catherine. I wanted to believe you when you said you wouldn't publish the fact that Jody was my half-sister...but I was torn with doubts about you. It seemed a good idea at the time to just let you leave and then wait and see what happened.'

'A kind of test as to how low I would stoop?' Her words had a bitter ring.

'Yes, I suppose it was,' he admitted quietly. 'When you wrote nothing at all I could hardly believe it.'

'So now you are feeling suitably guilty that you might have judged me overly harshly? That perhaps you shouldn't have bedded me in quite such a cold-blooded, calculating way.' Her words were deliberately crude as she struck out at herself as well as him.

'It wasn't quite like that, was it, Catherine?'

'Wasn't it?' For a moment her voice held a tremor of pain.

Then she turned from him and started to walk away. 'I'm not interested in your apology and I'm not interested in interviewing you. Get someone else.'

'I don't want anyone else.'

'For God's sake, Pearce.' She spun to face him, her breath ragged, her anger acute. Then she stopped as a sudden wave of light-headedness swept over her. She felt very hot and for a frightening few seconds she wondered if she was going to faint.

'Catherine?' He was beside her in an instant, his arm going around her to support her. 'What is it? Aren't you well?'

'I'm fine.' She tried to push him away but her limbs were weak. Perhaps it was just the fact that she had turned too quickly, or perhaps the fact that her stomach was empty, or that her anger had lifted her blood pressure. Whatever the reason, she felt frightened by the dizziness...the feeling of not being in control.

'Come on, I'll take you home.'

She didn't argue with him. It was a relief to be supported by him.

'Can you walk?'

She nodded. 'I'm all right, Pearce. If you'll just come with me to my front door…it's not far.'

'I know where it is.'

For a moment her lips curved at his quiet assurance. 'Ah, yes, I was almost forgetting that you had a detailed file drawn up on me.'

'I know almost everything there is to know about you, Catherine,' he said with a small smile.

'Not everything,' she assured him quietly.

They stopped by the entrance to Cathy's apartment block and he watched as she took her front door key from her bag. 'I'll be fine now,' she told him, trying to get some of her old brisk confidence back into her voice, but it wobbled precariously.

'I'll come up with you.' He took the key firmly from her hand.

It seemed strange, having Pearce in her apartment. She had spent so many weeks trying not to think about him and now suddenly here he was.

She sat down on one of the leather sofas in the lounge as he went through to the kitchen to get her a drink of water.

'Do you feel any better?' he asked after she had taken a few sips of the cool liquid.

She nodded. 'Sorry, I think I'm just overtired.' She felt obliged to make some kind of excuse. 'I've been working very hard recently.'

She wondered what he would say if she told him the truth—that she was expecting his baby? Her eyes moved thoughtfully over his tall, broad-shouldered frame. He would be very shocked. He would probably even offer to help her with money. She pushed a hand through her hair. She didn't want his money, and she didn't think she could bear to have him on the sidelines of her life. It would be like torture, seeing him but not having him. Just like this was torture.

'Trying to make up for the Tyrone disaster interview?' he asked now and grinned.

'Something like that.' She looked away from him down at the glass in her hand. 'How's Poppy?' She was aware of a lump in her throat as she asked that question. She thought of Poppy often. Sometimes in her blackest moments of despair, when she considered not going ahead with this pregnancy, it was the memory of Poppy's wide blue eyes and sunny smile that pulled her sharply away from such an option.

'She's well and happily back with her mother.'

'So Jody has completely recovered, then?'

'More or less. She's resting at my villa for a while.'

'That will cause a stir of interest amongst the press, won't it?' she asked stiffly.

'Probably.' He sounded unconcerned. 'I suppose the truth will be out any day now anyway.'

She put her glass down on the table next to her. 'Well, I haven't said anything.'

'I know. But I've thought about what you said to me. It's too big a secret to keep for long. Jody and I have discussed it and she agrees with me...' He shrugged. 'I can't keep up a silence about it for much longer... It makes my life—my relationships—too hard.'

Cathy wondered if he was talking about his relationship with Laura. 'I thought you said that the truth about Jody could hurt a lot of people?'

'I thought it could... I was worried mostly about the effect it would have on my mother.' He turned from her and stood staring out of the window at the quayside below.

'You see, I only discovered that I had a half-sister when my father was dying two years ago. Perhaps you can imagine my shock when he confessed to having had an affair twenty-five years ago and then told me that I had a sister I knew nothing about?'

'It must have been like a bombshell,' Cathy said quietly.

'Yes. Apparently the affair didn't last very long. My father realised his mistake...he loved my mother and didn't want his marriage to end. But he always provided for Jody and took the responsibility very seriously. They had a good relationship.'

The thought flitted briefly through her mind that Pearce would probably be the same with any child of his. Her heart thudded unevenly. Not telling him about the baby was probably doing a vast injustice to her child. The moment the notion crossed her mind she dismissed it. She knew she couldn't cope with a situation where Pearce was married to someone else...possibly Laura...having children with Laura but still coming here on birthdays and holidays. The very idea made her blood run like ice in her veins.

'And your mother still doesn't know about it?'

'I thought she didn't.' He turned to look at her. 'Until recently, when she rang me up to tell me that she was glad that I was looking after Poppy. Then it just all came out. Apparently she had known the truth and forgiven my father for it years ago.'

'But they had never talked about it?'

'I think each was too frightened of hurting the other,' His lips twisted ruefully. 'The tragedy was that neither realised just how strong their marriage really was—how deep their love really was for each other—until it was too late for talking.'

There was silence for a moment as he looked at her. There was a sadness on his face that made Cathy want to get up and put her arms around him. She bit down on the softness of her lip. It wasn't her place to comfort him. He had Laura and probably any number of other women in his life. She didn't want him here, she told herself furiously. He stirred up too many emotions, too many needs, inside her.

'So, why exactly are you telling me all this, Pearce?' Her voice was sharp with impatience—against herself, against him. 'You surely don't want me to write about it?'

'Yes, I do. Both my mother and Jody have said that they would like the story to come out in an accurate and sensitive way... I think they reckon that it's only a matter of time before some member of the press gets hold of it. So perhaps it would be better to collaborate on it now...make sure it's told well.'

So that was why he was here. She took a deep breath. 'And, as I already know that Jody is your sister, you thought I was the best person to approach?'

'Something like that.'

She got up from the sofa. 'I can't do it, Pearce.'

'What do you mean, you can't do it? I thought you would jump at the chance.'

'Well, you thought wrong.' Cathy glared at him.

'I don't understand you, Cathy.'

The quietly spoken remark made her heart jump. She didn't understand herself very much at this moment. All she knew was that it was too painful to be around Pearce. She knew very well from past experience that there was no way she could deal with anything to do with him in an objective manner...her emotions were too tightly intertwined.

'You can get someone else to do it.'

'I've told you I don't want someone else.'

'Well, I'm not going to do it, Pearce, so that is up to you.' There was a determined spark in her eyes.

'Fair enough.' He shrugged. 'If you don't want to do it, we'll leave it.'

She hadn't expected him to back down quite so easily. She stared at him with scepticism.

He smiled. 'So, how about dinner tonight?'

Her eyes narrowed. 'I'm not going to change my mind, Pearce.'

He laughed. 'It makes a change for me to be the one trying to coerce you into writing an article, doesn't it?'

'It is a bit ironic,' she agreed stiltedly. She didn't like it when he smiled at her like that. When he had that warm look in his eyes she felt her insides turning over. She wanted him so much...wanted to go into his arms.

'I promise that if you come out to dinner with me I won't mention newspaper articles once.' He held up a hand, a gleam of teasing humour in his eyes.

'So, what will we talk about, then?' Her voice was cold as she fought against the temptations he aroused so easily.

'Anything you want to talk about. The weather...you and me.'

'Sounds like a short conversation,' she said bleakly. 'It's cold for the time of year. You think I'm a hard, unscrupulous journalist and I think you are a womaniser and a rat.'

'Come on, Catherine.' His voice dropped to a velvet softness. 'Give me a chance.'

'A chance for what?' Her heart bounded against her chest. She had to keep reminding herself of how cold he had been that afternoon after they had made love...how little it had meant to him. He was a heart-breaker. Why she hadn't recognised the signs before, she didn't know. Perhaps she had just been blinded by the fact that he was so good with Poppy—so caring, so loving. Her heart thudded even more furiously at that memory.

'A chance for us to start over fresh. We have no secrets between us now, nothing to get in the way.'

'In the way of what?' Her eyes narrowed on him.

'You charming me into writing your story...or seducing me into your bed?' Her voice trembled alarmingly. 'What's the matter? Isn't Laura free for dinner tonight?'

He frowned. 'Laura is in New York. We had dinner before she left but—'

'Well, then, you'll just have to wait for her to come back. Won't you?' She marched to her front door and held it open. 'I'm busy, Pearce. In fact, I've got a date myself tonight.'

'With whom?' There was nothing gentle about his voice now.

Her mind went blank. 'David Collins.' The fact that David was still in the South of France was irrelevant. He would suffice.

'David Collins, that reporter in France...?'

'That's the one.' Cathy's voice was flippant.

'Tell me, was he the man you were once engaged to?'

The quietly asked question made her feel very uncomfortable. 'Yes.'

'So, are you two getting back together, then?'

'Probably.'

'I thought you said you had very little in common...that he didn't even like children and you—'

'For heaven's sake, Pearce.' She cut across him furiously: 'This is none of your business.'

There was anger on the handsome face, then he shrugged. 'You're right, none of my business.'

Then quietly he walked out of the door.

CHAPTER THIRTEEN

CATHY studied her reflection in her bedroom mirror. The plain black dress was stylishly elegant. It clung to her slender waist and then dropped almost to the floor. She wore no jewellery to adorn the square-cut neckline but her hair was loose in a soft feminine flow of gold around her shoulders.

She would pass, she decided critically as she put just a touch more blusher on the smooth paleness of her skin.

Attending the literary dinner at Clarins Hotel had been Mike's idea. He had tossed the invitation across her desk almost as a challenge.

'How did you get this invitation?' she had asked suspiciously. 'They must be like gold dust.'

'I'm not without my literary connections.' He had smiled, very pleased with himself. 'You can write all about it for your column next week.'

'And, of course, Pearce Tyrone will be there,' she had said softly.

'Of course.'

She had left it at that. She hadn't told Mike that she had refused to write the article about Tyrone and Jody Sterling. On the contrary, she had told her boss that she had seen Tyrone and had allowed him to believe that she was working on an article.

It was a week since she had seen Pearce. And once her emotions had started to settle—once she had calmed down just a little—she had realised her mistake in refusing to write the story that he had offered her.

For one thing, Mike knew that Tyrone had made himself available for an interview and he would never forgive her if she didn't take the scoop that was being offered. She had probably been a fool, hesitating so long. If, next week, the full story was to appear in a rival newspaper she would probably lose her job…her reputation as a good journalist.

That was the reason she hadn't argued with Mike about going with him to the dinner this evening. It would be a chance to see Pearce, have a quiet word with him and tell him that she had changed her mind.

It was just work, she told herself briskly. She had her career, her future, her baby to think about. It would take a couple of hours at most to interview Pearce, get all the details and then she could forget it all and get on with her life.

The doorbell rang. Suppressing a shiver of apprehension, Cathy picked up her evening bag.

Clarins was an elegant palatial hotel on the banks of the river Thames. The dinner was held in a large ballroom that seated over three hundred guests. Consequently Cathy didn't see Pearce until after the meal was finished and the awards ceremony began. And then it was only a fleeting glimpse as he went up on stage to collect an award for his latest book.

He was dressed in a dark dinner suit and he looked fabulously attractive. He said just a few brief words, thanking people, then he sat down again.

Cathy couldn't see who he was sitting with—he was too far away. She could see that he was seated at a large table where everyone seemed to know him.

Suddenly her idea about having a quiet word with him seemed ludicrous and she couldn't wait to get away.

When the awards came to an end and everyone stood up to adjourn to the lounges for drinks she glanced at her watch. 'It's getting rather late—'

'Nonsense, the night is young.' Mike grinned at her

and linked his arm firmly through hers. 'There are a few
people I must talk to. Let's get a drink.'

The room was crowded and hot. Thankfully Cathy
found herself standing in a space next to the open doors
which led out onto the terrace.

Mike thrust a glass of champagne into her hand and
then introduced her to a group of people he seemed to
know very well. Cathy smiled politely, then her eyes
searched the room.

Chandeliers blazed over the sophisticated gathering.
Diamonds flashed at the throats of fashionably pallid
women. Even the conversations sounded overly bright.

Then across the room she saw Pearce. He was surrounded by people but she could see that there was a
woman with him, her arm linked through his. She was
very attractive, with dark shining hair and a figure that
any woman would envy. Cathy expected it to be Laura
Houston. But as the woman turned slightly she saw that
it was not. It was someone Cathy had never seen before.

Surprise was closely followed by a fierce thrust of
jealousy as the woman stood on tiptoe and kissed the
side of Pearce's cheek. He smiled at her then, glancing
up, his eyes met Cathy's.

She looked away and tried to concentrate on the conversation going on around her. But her mind wouldn't
oblige.

'It's very hot in here, isn't it?' she said to Mike when
she had his attention for a brief moment.

'It's a very warm evening.' He shrugged. 'Would you
like another drink?'

She shook her head. 'If you don't mind, I think I'll
just step out onto the terrace for a breath of fresh air.'

'No...I don't mind.'

Cathy put her untouched drink down on a table and
hastily moved out of the crowds.

It was a relief to be outside. The terrace was deserted

and it had a wonderful view out over the river and the lights of the city. It was a lovely evening, there was hardly a ruffle in the dark water of the Thames and a languid summer heat hung over everything.

'Summer has arrived at last.'

Pearce's voice made her turn anxiously.

He was alone, and she wasn't sure if she was grateful for that or not. She watched as he put his glass down on one of the tables and then crossed to stand next to her at the stone balustrade.

'It is a lovely evening,' she commented, more for something to say than anything else.

'Well, that is the weather dispensed with.' His voice was jovial. 'What did I say we could talk about after that?'

Cathy swallowed hard. She knew full well that he was referring to his invitation to have dinner and the fact that she had said that there was nothing for them to talk about. 'Congratulations on your award,' she said lightly, hoping to deflate the tense atmosphere.

'Thank you. I hate these things, really. I don't usually come.'

'You looked as if you were enjoying yourself.' Cathy tried to keep the bitterness from her tone. She had no right to be jealous, she told herself crossly. She had no claim on Pearce Tyrone. She glared out across the lights of the city. 'Who is your new girlfriend?'

'I'll introduce you later, if you like.'

She could hear the jesting note in his voice and for some reason it made her angry.

'No, thank you.' She hoped that her voice wasn't as stiff and resentful as she felt.

'You are full of surprises... I thought you might like to interview her.'

There was a brief moment of silence. Cathy didn't dare to look at him, her eyes were staring at a distant point of light. She felt like a tightly coiled spring, ready to pull apart at any moment. Of course she had said the wrong thing. She was supposed to be telling him that she was interested, that she had changed her mind about the interview. She should have realised that keeping her professional cool was impossible around him... Wouldn't she ever learn that lesson?

'Where's you boyfriend tonight?'

'You mean David Collins?' She asked the question lightly, in an attempt to make it sound as if she had more than one boyfriend. She couldn't bear the thought that he might realise she was jealous. That would be the final humiliation.

'That's exactly who I mean.' His voice held an edge now, as if she was cutting through the banal, jesting mood and starting to irritate him.

'Oh...he had to work tonight.'

'Where?'

The question made her blink in surprise. 'I don't know, some...some function that he was asked to cover.' She didn't have the faintest clue where David was these days.

'In London?'

'Yes...yes, of course,' she snapped, uncomfortable with lying to him.

'So you will be seeing him later?'

'I don't know...maybe.' She shook her head. 'What's with all the questions, Pearce? Anyone would think you were jealous.'

'Just interested.'

His cool manner inflamed her raw senses. Of course Pearce wouldn't be jealous. To feel an emotion like that you had to care.

'What about Laura?' She took a deep breath and tried to bring her voice back to a civil, normal tone. 'I thought she would have been here with you tonight.'

'Laura's in the South of France.'

'She gets around, doesn't she? New York last week, now France again.'

'She is seeing someone in France. I think it could be serious.'

Cathy turned to look at him then, her interest aroused. 'Are you bothered?'

'Bothered? Why should it affect me?' He sounded totally surprised by the question.

'Well, I thought that you and Laura... I thought you liked her.' Cathy mumbled, feeling confused.

'I do—as a friend and a colleague, nothing deeper than that.' He shook his head. 'No, it's you that it should bother.'

She frowned, not following him at all.

'Seeing that the person Laura is so involved with is David Collins. Apparently he has been there all this time, has never, in fact, been back in England at all.'

She felt her face flood with heat at those softly spoken words. Her heart thumped unsteadily, its beat filling her eardrums.

'You lied to me, Cathy,' he murmured and reached out a hand to touch her face. 'Why did you lie?'

The touch of his hand against her skin sent a flare of longing shooting through her.

'I...I don't know.' She didn't know what to say, what even to think.

'Should I guess? Were you perhaps trying to make me jealous?' His voice was soft, making all her senses spin in confusion.

'No... Why would I want you to be jealous?' She stepped back from him, as if putting a little space between them might break the spell he cast over her. She desperately needed a return to realism. She was starting to be ruled by emotion, just like every other time when she had come into close contact with Pearce.

'I've asked myself that a few times since I discovered that Collins was in France.'

'Look, why don't you go back inside to your girl-friend and leave me alone?' Her panic was starting to show in her voice. 'You are a womaniser, Pearce, a no-good heart-breaker and I'm not—'

'Come on.' He caught hold of her arm. 'Come and say hello to my girlfriend.'

'Pearce, stop it.' She tried to pull away from him, but he was much stronger and much more determined. Short of making a scene in the room, she had to follow him into the lounge and across the crowded floor.

'Catherine...' He tugged her further forward until she was face to face with the attractive brunette. 'I'd like you to meet Jody.'

Cathy's eyebrows lifted. 'Jody Sterling?' Now that she was up close she could see that it was indeed Jody. The girl was frail and thin-looking and she had a jagged scar over one side of her forehead which she had tried to hide skilfully with make-up and a new hairstyle. She had changed her hair colour, too.

Jody laughed and touched her hair ruefully. 'No one has recognised me since I've changed my hair.'

'Oh!' Cathy felt totally foolish now. She flicked an uncertain glance at Pearce, wondering if she had sounded as jealous as she had felt.

'Are you Catherine Fielding?' Jody asked suddenly.
Cathy nodded.

'I want to thank you for looking after Poppy for me,' the girl said sincerely. 'Pearce told me how wonderful you were.'

'Did he?' Cathy was totally dazed now. Before she could say anything else, or ask the girl how she was feeling, Pearce interrupted. 'Look, Jody, I'm going to go now. I've got a few things to sort out with Catherine.'

'I'm sure you have.' Jody slanted a knowing smile at

Cathy, then back again at her brother. 'Are you going back to the house?'

He nodded.

'OK, I won't hurry home. Just check on Poppy for me, though.'

'Look, Pearce, I can't go anywhere with you.' Cathy felt breathless as he proceeded to lead her away from his sister towards the lobby of the hotel. 'I'm with Mike.'

'Mike will understand. He knew the only reason he got an invitation tonight was so that I could see you.'

'You mean you arranged for us to be here?'

'Of course. I thought it was the only way I'd get a chance to speak to you. You were so damn cold and standoffish the other day.'

As they moved out onto the street Pearce lifted his hand to get a taxi. One stopped immediately and he opened the door for her to get in.

'You do realise that Mike is never going to let up about you now...' Cathy's voice was stiff. She settled herself in the back of the cab and glared at him.

'Well, write the damn article and then forget about him,' Pearce answered calmly.

'Is that the reason you've manoeuvred me here tonight?' Her voice rose sharply. 'Because, if it is, let me tell you that you didn't need to go to such trouble. I've changed my mind. I've decided to write your article.'

'I knew you'd come to your senses eventually.' He grinned at the look of outrage on her face.

'Well, it was either that or look for another job,' she told him in no uncertain terms.

'You'd always land another job.'

'Thanks for the vote of confidence,' she muttered, unconvinced. 'But after failing with your story I reckon I'd be lucky if I got a job as a nanny.'

'Well the Dubonnet family would probably give you a reference.'

Despite everything, she smiled and suddenly she felt herself relax. 'That was a real give-away...wasn't it?'

'If I hadn't already known I would have done then,' he agreed.

Their eyes met and he reached out a hand and took hers. 'You're very beautiful, do you know that?' His voice was like silk to her senses. She swallowed hard.

'And you're a charmer, Pearce Tyrone.' Her voice was husky.

The taxi pulled up outside a tall Georgian town house and Pearce paid the driver before leading the way out into the street.

'Is this yours?' Cathy asked, looking up at the impressive red-brick house.

'Yes...I never stay long. I prefer to be in France.'

He led the way inside.

It was a stylish house, furnished with tasteful elegance.

There was a young woman in her late teens in the lounge, reclining on one of the squashy sofas—a book in her hands. She stood up as she heard them come in.

'How was Poppy?' Pearce asked her with a smile.

'Fine, Mr Tyrone. Not a sound out of her all night.' The girl slanted an inquisitive look at Cathy.

'Thanks, Natalie.' Pearce pulled out his wallet to pay the girl and then went to see her out of the front door.

'My next-door neighbour's daughter,' Pearce said as he came back. 'She's handy for babysitting when Jody visits.'

'I think she was rather surprised to see that you had gone out with a brunette and returned with a blonde,' Cathy said with a wry twist of her lips.

'Well, I've got my reputation to uphold, haven't I?' he said with a laugh.

'What reputation is that?'

'The one the papers are fond of portraying at the moment.' He slanted her a dry look. 'The one you were flinging at me not so long ago... How does it go— womaniser and rat?'

'Oh.' Her face flared with colour. 'Well...I thought you were two-timing Laura...' She shrugged awkwardly. 'How was I to know you were out with your sister? You told me that she was at your villa.'

'She was. She's just here for a few days.' He looked at her with a serious light in his eyes. 'Were you truly so upset because you thought I was two-timing Laura?'

'I wasn't upset.' She denied the accusation staunchly.

'You sounded upset.'

'Well, I wasn't. She glared at him, her heart thumping. She had her pride. She would never admit how jealous she had felt about Jody...about Laura.

'I'd better go and check on Poppy.' Pearce's voice was suddenly heavy. 'Help yourself to a drink.' He nodded towards the drinks cabinet, then left the room.

For a moment Cathy stood indecisively. She didn't want a drink. What she did want was a glimpse of Poppy. She hesitated and then followed Pearce from the room.

He was at the top of the stairs and he looked down as he heard her in the hall.

'I though I'd have a little look at Poppy,' she murmured. 'Do you mind?'

He shook his head and waited for her to join him on the landing.

'Almost like old times, isn't it?' He smiled at her and then opened the door into the nursery.

A night-light lit a room that was decorated in dreamy pastel shades of pink and blue. In a corner, in her cot, Poppy was fast asleep.

Cathy looked down at the little girl and a surge of

love filled up inside her. 'She's grown,' she whispered tenderly as she tucked the sheet around her and then watched the steady rise and fall of her breathing.

'She has two more teeth, would you believe?'

'Really?' Cathy smoothed back the soft blonde curls with a gentle hand.

'Do you remember the day you arrived when she wouldn't stop crying?'

Cathy looked across at Pearce. 'I'll never forget it.'

Suddenly the memories...the atmosphere...was more than Cathy could bear. She moved back from the cot. 'I...I'd better go, Pearce.' She turned for the door, but he caught up with her before she could go out.

'Catherine, don't go.'

She looked back at him, here eyes misting with tears. 'Look, Pearce, I've said that I'll do that article. I don't know why it's so important to you that I—'

'Hell, Catherine, I couldn't give a damn about any article.' His voice was a low husky sound in the silence of the nursery. 'It's you I want... It's always been you that I wanted. I was a fool to let you walk out of my life and I've missed you every damn day since.'

She wiped a tear from the cool pallor of her skin, her hand trembling as she stared at him in disbelief.

'You told me you weren't jealous about me...but I've been eaten alive with jealousy over you.' He put a hand on her shoulder. 'That day when David Collins arrived on my boat I wanted to hit him...' his mouth curled in a derisive dry line...'when I saw the way he looked at you—the way he followed you about—and I realised that he was the person you were working with and probably the person that you were romantically involved with.'

Cathy shook her head, hardly able to believe what he was saying.

'When Laura and David had left us I couldn't contain

myself... I wanted you, Catherine... I wanted you so badly that it hurt.'

She was shaking now, trembling with reaction.

'I still want you now,' he said softly. 'I want to take you to bed and make love to you, make you mine.' He stroked her blonde hair away from her face with a tender hand. 'I want it to be unhurried this time, Catherine... I—'

'Stop...stop it.' She took a deep breath. 'This is just sex, Pearce.' She shook her head, willing herself to control the tempestuous desire he was able to arouse in her. She had regretted giving in to that desire last time... He had made her feel so used...so cheap. The pain of it was there now. It made her so afraid, so hurt inside.

'Just sex?' He ground the words out as if they were beneath contempt, and then he kissed her. It was a passionate kiss. It drugged her senses, making her feel rather than think. It made her cling to him in need of more.

She loved him, she loved him so much that she felt dizzy with it.

When finally he pulled away he looked down at her with a tender smile. 'It's not just sex, Catherine... It's the real thing and I've been fighting it since I first set eyes on you.'

'Really?' Her voice shook with emotion.

'Really.' He kissed her lips again and then the side of her face, and his arms held her close against his body.

'Do you remember that evening when you said that my protective instinct was to back away from deep involvement? That I was afraid of losing the woman I loved the way I lost my wife?'

'Yes.' Cathy remembered how she had accused him of that in an attempt to get him to admit to his real feelings for Jody.

'Well, you were right... Oh, not about Jody, of

course.' He held her tightly. 'But I have been afraid to get involved... I have hidden myself away since my wife died...' He sighed. 'When you arrived out of nowhere on my front doorstep I was instantly smitten... I felt something for you that baffled me, it was so instant. But I told myself that I was letting you stay because I wanted to play the game...see where it would lead.'

He held her away from him and looked down into her eyes. 'It was an excuse, Catherine. I wanted you to stay. Then, when we kissed, I told myself it was not serious, but that was an excuse.'

'And then we made love and you told me that you just wanted to see how far I would go...?' Her voice was numb.

'I was lying to myself, Catherine.' He shook his head. 'Even when I let you walk out of my house, I was still lying to myself. I think that even when I rang the paper and asked to see you for lunch I was still trying to play a game and tell myself it was just to make amends with you...give you an interview.'

'And now?' She pulled away from him.

'And now I've run out of excuses.' He raked an unsteady hand through his hair. 'Catherine, I love you... I need you. Every day without you is a bad day.'

She smiled tremulously through her tears.

'Will you marry me, Catherine?' The softly asked question made her heart miss a beat. She wiped a hand over the paleness of her cheeks, smoothing away the tears.

'It's not really as simple as that.'

He frowned. 'Is there someone else?'

'In a way.' Her voice was low and uncertain.

'Hell, Catherine, it's not David, is it? I thought when I found out that you had been lying to me about him—'

'Yes, I was.' She shook her head dismissively. 'There

hasn't been anything between David and I for a very long time.'

'So, who?' He sounded angry, distraught almost, and she smiled just for a moment before her anxiety returned. She looked at him shyly.

'I'm pregnant, Pearce... I'm going to have your baby.'

If she hadn't been so anxious the look of stunned amazement on his face might have made her laugh. 'You don't mind?' she whispered, half fearful, half hopeful.

'Mind?' He looked at her in astonishment and then he gathered her up in his arms and kissed her. 'Catherine, I'm overwhelmed with happiness.'

Suddenly she was crying, holding onto him and weeping.

He held her tenderly. 'Hush, my darling. I love you...everything will be fine.'

'I know, that's why I'm crying.' She buried her head against his shoulder. 'Oh, Pearce I love you so much.'

'Come into my room and tell me that.' He growled the words seductively against her ear. Then quietly they closed the door on the sleeping baby.

Take 4 bestselling love stories FREE

Plus get a FREE surprise gift!

**Make a Valentine's date
for the premiere of**

◆ HARLEQUIN® **Movies**

starting February 14, 1998 with

Debbie Macomber's
This Matter of
Marriage

on

Just tune in to **The Movie Channel** the **second Saturday night** of every month at 9:00 p.m. EST to join us, and be swept away by the sheer thrill of romance brought to life. Watch for details of upcoming movies—in books, in your television viewing guide and in stores.

If you are not currently a subscriber to The Movie Channel, simply call your local cable or satellite provider for more details. Call today, and don't miss out on the romance!

100% pure movies.
100% pure fun.

◆ HARLEQUIN®
*M*akes any time special.™

An Alliance Production   HMBPA298

shocking pink

THEY WERE ONLY WATCHING...

The mysterious lovers the three girls spied on were engaged in a deadly sexual game no one else was supposed to know about. Especially not Andie and her friends whose curiosity had deepened into a dangerous obsession....

Now fifteen years later, Andie is being watched by someone who won't let her forget the unsolved murder of "Mrs. X" or the sudden disappearance of "Mr. X." And Andie doesn't know who her friends are....

WHAT THEY SAW WAS MURDER.

ERICA SPINDLER

Available in February 1998 at your favorite retail outlet.

The Brightest Stars in Women's Fiction.™